HOLY WAR

by

Jonathan Farlow

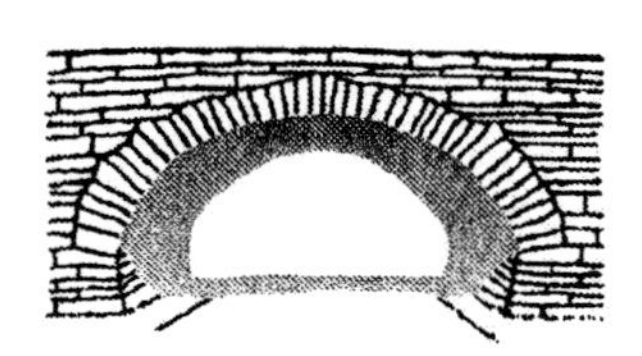

2004
Parkway Publishers, Inc.
Boone, North Carolina

Library of Congress Cataloging in Publication Data

Farlow, Jonathan, 1969-
Holy war / Jonathan Farlow.
p. cm.
ISBN 1-887905-83-9
1. Terrorism--Prevention--Fiction. I. Title.
PS3606.A7 H65 2004
813'.6--dc22
2003025060

Book Design by Aaron Burleson, Spokesmedia
Cover Illustration by Jim Fleri

To Kathy

Without you this book would have never
been written, or anything else for that matter.
I owe you a lot.

I love you,
Jon

I
A Fink in the Armor

Be strong! Be courageous!
Do not be afraid of them!
For the Lord your God will be with you.
He will neither fail you nor forsake you.
Deuteronomy 31:6

Who said I was Paranoid?!
Anonymous

You don't have to be very well read, very well informed, or very bright to realize that the events of the last year and a half have changed America forever. The tragedies of September 11th proved that the ivory tower that was the United States could be rocked and, although most of us heeded our country's leaders and did not change our way of life, we changed our way of thinking. Our priorities and our view of those things that we took for granted changed, at least for a month or two, and a nagging fear that bordered on paranoia for some crept into our mindset.

The scope and the gravity of the previously mentioned events as well as their aftermath can be judged by their effect on Welbourne County, North Carolina. Throughout the history of this little patch of red clay it has proven to have a sturdy, almost uncanny, resistance to the social and political upheavals of the outside world. This division from the world around it was for the most part voluntary and owing to the pride and thick-headed stubbornness of its people as well as simple rolls of the dice. There's a saying among the old-timers that most people in the county were so poor that, when the Great Depression started, they didn't even notice. During all the conflicts of this past century the combined lists of casualties from Welbourne County were limited to two during the Vietnam War and one Gerald "the Fink" Finkle, a naval Lieutenant in service during World War II who proved to be so obnoxious that his own men threw him overboard two days out of the Philippines in early 1944. Unbeknownst to all who knew him, the Fink lived for many years on a small uncharted atoll in the South Pacific. He was discovered by a Navy troop ship in 1971 and died on board on the way back to Hawaii.

Welbourne County's armor, however, was not thick enough to keep out the demons that fell from the sky on 9/11, and that same fear, that same dread that something like this might happen again, began to creep in and fester like an open sore until it all came to a head this past summer.

If you want to be particular about it, it all started when the Sheriff's Department raided that meth-house out on Adam's Ford Road in early April. Drugs, crime, and the filth that such poison brings with it was another evil of the outside world that occasionally (more and more often it seems) has crept in under the door. The raid was featured on the 11:00 news. Sheriff Leo Dorsey and his deputies took along a news crew from an affiliate in Winston-Salem. It was an election year and "Old Iron Britches," as Sheriff Dorsey is known around these parts, wanted the people of Welbourne County to see the lengths that he was going to "Crush that viper under his heel and send it back to the pit from where it came from." As he was quoted in *The Ashewood Falls Harbinger* the following day.

Sheriff Dorsey had taken a lot of flack for well over a year since an Ashewood Falls High School freshman was pulled off the house trailer that serves as the school's computer lab. He was buck naked, screaming something about his auto shop teacher being an assassin for the C.I.A. and, as discovered at Welbourne Memorial that night, stewed to the gills on crystal-meth. This was in contrast to what the Welbourne County Sheriff's department had assured the people of the county: That drugs had not reached their little part of the world; they were not circulating through the schools, and they hadn't gotten to their children.

Truth is that one of the county's earliest residents, Ashewood Bennett for whom the town of Ashewood Falls is named, found a bumper crop of marijuana growing on his land sometime in the late 1870's although he didn't know what it was until an Indian, the same Indian who had planted it there in the first place, identified it for him and introduced him to its euphoric qualities. He became an avid user and most people who knew him before then said it improved his behavior, coordination and personality. Mrs. Jacinda

Mann was also known to be an avid user of marijuana although she claimed that it was called hemp, was no relation to marijuana and, furthermore her physician had prescribed it to uncross her eyes. In more recent times the only well known citizen of Welbourne County to have had his own bout with drugs, or the only one to ever admit it, was our mayor, Johnston Farley, who confessed to developing a fondness for LSD while he was serving a tour of duty in Vietnam. The mayor had no trouble after he returned save one incident in early '78 when he hit Ruby Simpkins in the head with an umbrella because he saw Nikita Kruschev disappear into her beehive.

Within a week of the incident at the high school the people of the county went from wanting to lynch whoever was selling the mess to wanting to lynch the sheriff for letting them sell it. This was a threat to the sheriff's image as a hard-nosed, tough-on-crime old school southern sheriff who wore a tie tack shaped like a noose, had a miniature electric chair adorning his desk and showed up at public appearances brandishing an ax handle like Joe Don Baker in *Walking Tall.* It also threatened the easy life that the Sheriff had enjoyed for much of his twenty year stint in office. His popularity plummeted all through the next summer and seemingly took a shot through the head when one of his deputies, a transplanted Yankee named Keith Miller, announced that he would be running for Sheriff opposite Dorsey. For the first time in almost a decade "Old Iron Britches" would not run unopposed, and if the public sentiment that summer was any measure he would lose. In fact, he was sitting in his office running through a mental list of all the ways he would occupy his time when he was drummed out of office when an anonymous phone call informed the Sheriff of the location of one of two meth-labs which had been servicing the Welbourne County area for the last couple of years.

The first sting was relatively easy to carry out. After a few days of surveillance revealed almost an almost endless flow of traffic in and out of an old frame house out on Adam's Ford Road, a plain clothes detective was sent in and was able to purchase a gram of crystal meth as well as win ten dollars cash on video poker. After that, all it took was for Sheriff Dorsey and half a dozen other officers to bust in and shut the place down. Old Iron Britches went on camera within the hour to make it known that the sheriff's department had stopped the larger of two supplies of illegal drugs coming into the area and had all but crippled those forces who were trying to poison the children of Welbourne County. The camera then panned back to the house where a voiceover from the sheriff announced that those involved had been arrested, drugs and equipment had been confiscated and the house would be burned to the ground as practice for the local fire department. Any others involved in this operation faced the same fate.

The house was originally a toll house built in 1859 when one of the main roads for carriages and coaches ran through Adam's Ford, a small but bustling community even before there was a Welbourne County. Over the years the house passed through more owners than the supposed experts could count and it seemed that each one built on a room, extended walls and porches, raised ceilings and did whatever other do-it-yourself improvements that they could dream up, so by the time it was bought by one "Boochie" Owen, the owner at the time of the bust, the original house was encased in the rooms and add-ons that had been attached to it over the years. When it was photographed on the news and its fate was delineated by the sheriff, Francis Beck, a local historian and expert on the architecture of the county, recognized it as one of many buildings and houses that he had photographed for a book that he had written almost ten years before. Mr. Beck, an active and influential member of the Welbourne County Historical Society got on the phone to the present president of that organization, Mrs. Marilyn Misenheimer, and the call went out that the house, regardless of its recent history and the wishes of the sheriff's department, would be saved.

One day a week or two later Tony Dorsett, not the football player-the exterminator, pulled his puke green pickup truck, the one with a giant cockroach wearing a top hat welded onto the roof, up in front of the now famous house. The last he heard the Historical Society had said that they would pursue litigation to save the Toll House, as they called it, and had convinced some bureaucrat or other to let the society purchase it without the property even going to auction, which was the usual practice.

Tony had read about it all in the paper and swore that the house smelled funny as he crawled underneath it. All he knew was that Mayor Farley, who also owned Birddog Realty and was overseeing the purchase, called Tony and requested a termite inspection and, if necessary, pest removal treatment. He had hardly gotten out of the truck when Mrs. Misenheimer pulled in behind him and gave him a half hour lecture about how this house was of great historical value, that it just had to be saved and that she would accept nothing more than his best effort. She said that she had half mind to crawl underneath and check behind him, but Tony smiled at the mere thought of it and had no worries as he unloaded his equipment and went around back looking for the crawlspace door.

He had knelt down in front of the door, clicked on his flashlight and slid on his headphones. Tony always listened to music as he worked. It made the day pass faster. He hit the play button on his CD player and soon the bassy thump of gangsta rap was pounding in his ears. Long a country and classic rock aficionado, Tony had gotten into rap that summer. He had always liked Run-DMC's version of *Walk This Way* but he had never considered himself a rap fan until he started listening to Kid Rock because he looked like a good ol' redneck boy, which led him into other rap and hip-hop groups. The brand new *Ice Tre* album, *Honky: the Other White Meat,* was what he had been listening to that day, but, as he crawled around under the old Toll House, he had the radio on. Colin Powell had gone before the U.N. once again to talk about all the mess in Iraq and the President had just upgraded the terror alert level to Orange. Everybody knew that something was going to happen. It was just a matter of when and where. For Tony he couldn't stand the thought of something else like 9/11, but the wait was almost as bad. Day after day it was all he heard on the news, but nothing happened and Tony couldn't stand to be away from a radio or T.V. lest something should occur and he not know it.

If Tony could have had his way, the meth-house would have been as pristine and well built as the Biltmore House, but, alas, it wasn't. The boards underneath it were rotten to the point that he was surprised the house was standing at all. There was significant termite damage and evidence that there was rodent infestation as well. In layman's terms the place was "eat up with vermin," but Tony would have slammed his johnson in the truck door before he would tell Marilyn Misenheimer that. He crawled back out into the sunlight just as Tariq Aziz was vehemently denying, yet again, that Iraq had weapons of mass destruction.

"Yeah and my butt's a weed eater." Tony thought to himself as he walked to the truck. Mrs. Misenhemer had left her card with him and he had stuck it above the sun visor. He left it there however and called the mayor. He had his name on speed dial.

"She is going to hit the damn roof," the mayor said as soon as Tony had blurted out the bad news, "but you better call her."

"Mayor, don't you think that she would take it better coming from you, ya'll being acquainted and all?" Tony said as he propped the cell phone under his chin and opened a bottle of Gatorade. The mayor noticed a quiver in his voice that almost made it sound like he was whining. "Cause this is going to take some major repairs, if it can be fixed at all, and I don't think that group was talkin' about spending this kind of money."

"She isn't going to take it well, no matter who tells her." the mayor said, and it sounded like he took a big gulp of something to drink and maybe a puff on a cigarette. "So go ahead and call her. I'm just heading out and we need to get the bad news to her. It won't be pleasant for either one of us." Tony mumbled in agreement and hung up.

"Us hell," he griped as he got Marilyn's number down from the visor and called. Her son told him that she wasn't at home and that she would be gone for the rest of the day. He left a message for her to call the mayor and hung up. *"That's why he gets the big bucks,"* Tony thought to himself, slipped his headphones back on and took another swig of Gatorade. Just as he hit the switch on the Walkman he heard someone call from behind him toward the street. He looked that way and saw that a van had pulled into the driveway behind him, a rusty orange 70's era GMC disco mobile with a premiered front right fender, mag wheels and a little heart shaped window in the upper rear corner. The fella behind the wheel motioned him over, and, as the man's face became clear, the voices of thousands of war protestors were chanting into Tony's ears.

"No blood for oil! No blood for oil! No blood for oil!" As he got closer, he could see that the man was dark skinned with burning black eyes that stared out at him from beneath a "These colors don't run" baseball cap. He looked just like the people, save the cap, of course, you saw on the news burning the American flag in Pakistan or Syria, and all the rest of the men in the van, five in all, looked identical to the first save one who looked out at him from behind the driver's seat. He was a great deal younger and taller and where the others wore white t-shirts this one wore a Philadelphia 76's jersey. They all wore ball caps, the one in the back wore a blue one bearing Jeff Gordon's yellow number 24.

"Hep ya." Tony asked, sliding the headphones off his ears.

"I am looking for the hotel." The driver spoke and the rest of the men looked at Tony like he was naked from the waist down.

"Which hotel?"

"Any hotel. We are looking for a place to stay for the night."

"Well, if you stay on this road and make a right on 43, the

Motel Six is down there on the right. Take it on into town and get on McLean, there's a Holiday Inn downtown. Then there's the Hampton....."

"Where is nearest hotel."

"Well, there's the Cloud Nine. That's a mile or two down the road, but I don't think that's what ya'll are looking for." The words were hardly out of his mouth before the driver was cranking the engine and backing out into the road. Tony watched them go and then slid his headphones back onto his ears and, having heard enough of the Middle-East, war and violence, he cranked up Ice Tre.

II
"Down A Brew With Me Danny Boy!"

Daniel McDaniel has never been what you'd call a brave man. In fact he was as timid as a whore at a church social and he always thought, although he never told anybody, that his nerves were what led to his drinking problem. His mother always told him not to touch the stuff and he didn't. She drank, daddy drank, and his grandfather made it, but Daniel wouldn't even get near it for fear of Mama getting him. Welbourne County was dry then, so it wasn't like it was hard to stay away from booze. Mama had told Grandpa not to sell Danny any and, through him, the other bootleggers in the county agreed not to either. Then he went to Appalachian State University where the whiskey flowed like water and the yellow streak up his back worked against his abstinence rather than supporting it. Mama was a hundred miles away, and rather than show his anxiety or make a valid case for abstaining, Daniel just went along with the crowd although at first he likened the taste of whiskey to kerosene and beer to urine, although he had tasted neither. He warmed up to the taste in a big way, however, and real quick. He liked the way it made him feel. When he had a good snootful, he wasn't afraid anymore, he wasn't timid, he wasn't ashamed of who he was or what he thought. He still wasn't like all the jocks on campus who would down a few as fast as they could and then go looking for somebody to fight, but for the first time in his life he was confident, and although the ground was rolling beneath his feet, he strutted like a bantam rooster. He always planned to quit drinking when he graduated and had to become responsible, and he did as long as he was living at home, but as soon as he had gotten a job and saved enough money to get his own apartment and started hanging around with Wade Burgess again, who had been a crony in high school, the booze began to flow again. Wade was a drinker and made no bones about it. He also didn't care to be around anyone who wasn't. Daniel was still bringing in the few sticks of furniture that he owned when Wade, whom he had spoken to for the first time in years the day before, waltzed in with a case of Milwaukee's Beast, plopped down on the couch that Daniel had found out on the sidewalk, and set the beer down on the huge wooden spool that served as the coffee table until it caught fire a couple of months later.

"Down a brew with me Danny boy!" he had bellowed.

"No thanks." Daniel had said this with a firmness that he wasn't going to touch a drop. He was sure of himself, he was strong, he was a rock. He melted before Wade even finished his next sentence.

"Oh, grow a backbone. It'll put hair on your chest" His tone was commanding, almost indignant, and he threw the beer to Daniel with such force that it was either catch it or get knocked colder that the can. "You're a beer man; I can tell! Now drink up!" When Wade woke Daniel up sometime in the wee hours of the morning to tell him that he was leaving, he told him of a trashcan party that he was throwing the next day. Daniel took for granted that it would be at Wade's house and even bought a bottle of Evan Williams. When he got back home, Wade was waiting outside with the trashcan.

"I still live with Mama." Wade had said rather timidly.

Over the years Daniel 's battle with the bottle had been an ongoing struggle and he had varying degrees of success depending on the method, the reason and the timing of a particular lurch toward abstinence. Another key factor in Daniel's trips into and out of the bottle was his relationship with his "best friend" Wade, which was as rocky and troublesome as his relationship with alcohol. If he and Wade were as close as two peas then Daniel was a hopeless drunk, that even a bad car accident couldn't cure. When Wade had one of his famous tantrums, however, and put Daniel on one of his brown lists, then sobriety could be achieved easily, at least until Wade saw fit to let Daniel back into his good graces and the vicious cycle would start all over again.

Daniel quit for good this past summer. He was on the outs with Wade for shanking a 6-10 split and costing them the third game the last night of the Wednesday Night All Star League. They still won by a good amount and had won every other game, including total pins, that season; but it deflated Wade's ego to have the one loss. He made it known exactly whose fault it was as the Birddog Realty team celebrated six straight years as league champions in the Five-Pin lounge.

"We would have swept it all!" he said to somebody else, anybody who would listen, and made sure that Daniel could hear it. "If somebody hadn't missed that baby split! Yep, a perfect season ruined!" He continued a little later on in the evening when the first try didn't get a rise out of Daniel. "Maybe next year we should get T.J. Dorsett to bowl in Danny's Boy's place! He couldn't do any worse!" Daniel ordered another beer and nursed it until Wade started in again. "A good season shot to Hell!" was all he had to say before Daniel drained his glass, threw a few dollars down on the bar and headed out. As the door shut behind him, he could hear Wade's voice following him out. "Oh, let him go!"

Daniel stopped off at Kroger's on the way home from work, at the exact time that Tony was fishing AA batteries out from under his truck, having dropped his walkman. Daniel had picked up a case of Bud Light but, by the time he got to the house, he didn't feel like a beer. He cracked one open anyway, which wasn't unusual, sat down in front of the TV and started surfing through the channels looking for anything funny. He needed a laugh. The closest he could find was *Friends* so he settled for a Court TV documentary on Ted Bundy. What he wanted, what he needed was some company, somebody to talk to, but he knew that wasn't going to happen. His wife Lisa was working late again. Lisa, a buyer for Willow's Department Stores, had been gone so much over the last month that Daniel wasn't sure that he remembered what she looked like. A workaholic on a good day Lisa had been working late hours now that the Christmas season was just around the corner and had been going on buying trips, some lasting as much as a week, with her boss Mr. Collins, whom Lisa was certain pissed champagne. Daniel tried to wait up for Lisa to come home, but somewhere between Court TV and a biker movie with Joe Namath, Daniel killed the case and fell asleep in his easy chair. When he woke up, his head thumped like an old car was idling between his ears, his tongue had a quarter inch of fuzz on it, and his mouth tasted like he had just chugged a tall glass of stomach acid. Each sensation was far from new. In fact, mornings that he didn't wake up feeling like this was almost like he had slept in a strange bed. It just didn't feel right unless he felt like crap in the morning. The TV was still on and he lay there for a few minutes staring at Robert Osbourne announcing a Bowery Boys movie. He could hear someone moving around in the kitchen and forced himself to sit up and look around. It was Lisa dressed in her finest, as usual, when she was going off with Mr. Collins. She was filling her travel mug.

"Hey, sweetie." she said. "Sorry I woke you."

"You should have woke me up when you got home," he

answered struggling to his feet and walking toward her.

"Well, it was late and you were sleeping so good, all I did was come in and go to bed." She took a sip of coffee and started gathering up her purse and suitcase, which had been sitting at the end of the bar. "And now I'm off again. Sorry to say 'hey' and 'goodbye' but I've got to meet Mr. Collins at work. He's driving."

"Do you have to go? Didn't you just get back from one trip," He protested standing between her and the door.

"Well, I'm a buyer and this is a buying trip." Her tone was dripping with sarcasm, making him feel like a child who had just broken a window or something.

"It's Saturday; we're both supposed to be off. You said that the buying trip was in Raleigh; can't you just drive back and forth?"

"No, and we've been through this before. We finish up too late. I don't want to be driving back at two in the morning. Look," she put her hands on his shoulders and looked into his eyes. It was the first time in a long while that she had even touched him and he was right about forgetting what she looked like. Her eyes were brown, he could have swore they were blue. "It's something that just can't be helped. It's my job and that's all there is to it. We'll plan a trip or something after Christmas. That's the best I can do. Okay?"

"Sure." Daniel's tone was far from enthusiastic and he meant for it to sound that way, but it was lost on his wife.

"I'm late. I've got to go." She gave his shoulders a squeeze, no kiss, no hug, gathered her stuff and left. She poked her head back in the door and his heart leapt. "Hey, why don't you get a little work done on the bonus room?" Then she was gone again. He went to the kitchen window and watched her put her suitcase into the trunk and go. He couldn't remember when she had looked that nice. She was all made up, make-up, hair done, nice clothes, heels, and a skirt that cleared her knee by a good six inches. She hadn't looked that way since they had been married, well, not until the last year.

The McDaniel's house was part of the Oakton Estates subdivision that had grown up along the east side of Lake Ramsey in the late eighties. It was one of the choicest homes in the division, not because it was that much bigger or nicer than the rest, but because it sat not twenty yards from the water's edge. The house had a balcony which hung over the yard and was close enough to shore that Daniel could and sometimes did fish off it. Underneath was a concrete patio where they grilled out, or used to, and there was a tiny basement which could be accessed from a flight of stairs just off the den and opened onto the patio. It was Lisa's idea, right before she became Mr. Collins' right hand, or whatever part of the body she was, that they glass in the patio and knock down the wall to the basement making a large bonus room and another patio beyond closer to the water. Daniel wasn't crazy about the idea. He thought they had enough rooms and didn't need a bonus one, whatever that meant. He didn't warm up to the idea any more when Lisa said that it would be too expensive to hire someone and that Daniel could do it.

"You work in maintenance," she had told him. "You're good with your hands." The fact is Daniel wasn't good with his hands. He was head of the maintenance department at Woolman College which meant he attended meetings, did paperwork and left the manual labor for someone else. Lisa wouldn't hear of it; she started bringing home books on solariums, and do it yourself home improvement. "It's something you can be working on while I'm on these buying trips," she had told him and he had had plenty of time to work on them, but he really hadn't made much of an effort. Not that Lisa noticed.

After his wife was gone Daniel made himself a cup of coffee and went back to his chair to watch the 8 and 9 o'clock *Sportscenter*. Then, his head still aching, he filled the cup with whiskey, choked it down and went upstairs to get dressed. He brushed his teeth for a good five minutes and came back down with what tasted like a mouthful of bile and peppermint and went outside to stare at what he had already accomplished toward building the bonus room, which, again, wasn't much. He stared at one of the books that Lisa had gotten for him for a little while. This made his head feel worse, so he got a can of Budweiser out of the college size refrigerator in the basement.

He had already laid the frame for the floor and had started cutting boards for the floor itself when he last worked on it a week before. The boards were already measured, so he brought out the table saw and plugged it into an outlet set into one of the columns supporting the deck. Daniel had always been a little apprehensive around power tools, ever since Wade's shirt had been ripped off by a lathe in high school shop class. Today, however, he washed his apprehensions down with a beer and started sawing off boards to go from the outside frame and meet at a support in the middle. He was thinking about Lisa, which wasn't unusual, he always thought of her now that she was never around. He thought about how beautiful she had looked when she left and how he'd love to tell her that if she'd just come back for a minute or two. She had never dolled up for Daniel the way she had for Mr. Collins. He remembered the night a year before, almost to the day, that Lisa had come home so happy that she was practically dancing and informed him that she had been promoted from store manager to buyer. That day she had brought home what looked to be a whole new wardrobe in the trunk of her car and she just couldn't stop smiling. He eyes were big and bright and just couldn't stop dancing as she told her husband about her meeting with Mr. Collins when he had offered her the job. She hadn't been that happy in a long time. Then she started working late every so often, then a little more often, then these confound trips had started. It all pointed to the fact that Mr. Collins didn't want Daniel's wife for a right hand. In fact, he wasn't interested in her hands at all and, as giddy as she had been since she had started that job, it was becoming clear as time passed that Lisa was glad to give Mr. Collins whatever he wanted.

Daniel had been cutting boards with the mindless efficiency of a machine. When he again became aware of the world around him, he noticed that his face felt warm, that his heart felt like it was about to pound out of his chest, and that he was tossing 2 X 4's around like he was trying to break them rather than cut them. He had to calm down because his mouth immediately started sweating and he began to feel nauseated, so he closed his eyes and began breathing deeply, in through his nose out through his mouth, just as he started to push a board against the saw's spinning blade. He very slowly breathed in again through his nose but it was a good half minute before he would blow it out through his mouth because, at that moment, the saw blade neatly sliced off the tip of the middle finger on his left hand.

III
Gloom Despair And Agony On Me

Daniel spent a good four hours, his hand wrapped in his windbreaker, and tears running down his cheeks, sitting in the hospital waiting room between a woman with a wound similar to his own and a Mexican heaving into a styrofoam Biscuitville cup. The visit itself, where he got stitches into the end of his finger, a tetanus shot and a prescription for painkillers, lasted a little over an hour. It was almost four when he pulled out of the pharmacy drive-through, but it seemed like it should have been midnight at least. He stopped in at a drive through package store for another case and, while he was in line, the jerk in a big pickup truck behind him kept blowing a tractor-trailer style air horn every time the line crept forward. When they both had pulled into traffic and were making their way down 601, the truck pulled beside Daniel and the driver's side window rolled down. It was Wade Burgess.

"Danny boy," he bellowed. "Where're you going in such a hurry!" He took a minute to ponder Daniel with that pompous scornful gaze of his. "You looked like somebody licked the sweet off your sucker!"

"I cut my finger doing some work at the house."

"That was stupid!" Daniel showed Wade his cut middle finger, gunned the engine, and left him there on the highway. He was the last person that Daniel wanted to deal with right then and, as he vanished into traffic, he could see Wade mouth something in his direction before he turned off and went on his merry way.

As soon as Daniel got home, he went to the phone, and, taking out his wallet, leafed through the rat's nest of receipts, Post It's and scribbles of notes. It took him a good five minutes to find Lisa's cell phone number and then it rang for a good minute more. He was just about to hang up; he wanted to talk to his wife, not listen to James Earl Jones telling him she wasn't there, when Lisa picked up the phone. She seemed to struggle with it for a few seconds and then muttered a breathless "Hello."

"You all right?" Daniel muttered. "You sound out of breath."

"It's okay," She stopped like she was catching her breath. "I had to run for the phone. What's up?"

"I had a little accident. I cut my finger with the table saw."

"Are you all right?" She seemed to have caught her breath and sounded genuinely concerned. That made Daniel's finger hurt less and a warm feeling start to stir around in the pit of his stomach.

"Yeah, I just sliced off the tip of my devil finger."

"Baby, you have got to be careful with those power tools. But you're all right?"

"I guess. When are you coming home?"

"It'll be a few days. You can take care of yourself, can't you?"

"Yeah, sure." The warm feeling that Daniel had felt started bleeding out through his toes. He could hear someone talking in the background over the phone.

"Hold on a second," Lisa said, and he could hear muffled voices and laughter like she had put the phone against her hand or body. When she came back on the line, she was still giggling like some love struck school girl.

"Listen, I'll see you in a day or two. Take care of yourself."

"Bye." She didn't even say goodbye, just hung up and, as Daniel slapped the receiver back down onto the base, he did a mocking impression of his wife as he struggled to open his pill bottle.

"Oh Mr. Collins, you're so wonderful! Oh, thank you for the opportunity that you've given me! You won't be disappointed! I promise!" He popped two pills into his mouth without even looking at the label, took a beer from the case on the counter and washed them down. He went to his recliner, nursed his beer, stared at his finger and felt sorry for himself. His father always called it "playing poor soul" and every time Wade and the boys from the bowling team caught him doing it, they would always break into an off key rendition of the song from Hee Haw: "Gloom, despair and agony on me! Deep dark depression excessive misery!"

With Wade doing the exaggerated "Whoa Whoa's" at the end of each line, it always pissed him off, but they thought it was funny. This time though he didn't have the Hee Haw chorus, or his Daddy to tell him to pick up his lip and find something to do or even a wife to put his arm around or kiss his finger, so he just took turns looking at his wound and staring out the sliding glass door toward the lake. The sky had been a little overcast during the morning and had grown gloomier as the day wore on. As Daniel had been driving home, a fine mist had clung to the windshield and now, as he sat in his chair waiting for the painkillers to work, the world outside had turned a light shade of gray. The sky, the water, the opposite shoreline, even the air itself, was a uniform shade. He had no lights on in the house so the only illumination was coming through the glass doors, giving the inside of the house a gray hue as well.

The drops on the window pane had just started getting bigger when Daniel drained his beer and clicked on the T.V. He surfed around for a little while before settling on *America's Funniest Home Videos*. He still hadn't found the laugh he was looking for the night before. He got up to get another beer when something caught his eye. The table saw was still out in the back yard and it was starting to rain even harder. He didn't want to go outside and get wet, he wanted another beer, he wanted a good laugh, he wanted his wife, but he didn't want the saw to get ruined, and he was sure that it was still plugged up so he staggered toward the basement door. He had gone a few steps to the oval throw rug in the center of the room when he got real dizzy. He guessed that the painkillers were kicking in and, for the first time, saw the error in chasing them with beer. He stared down at the rug which appeared to be spinning so much that it looked like one of those spirals that hypnotists use to put their subjects under and it was making him even more dizzy. He looked up and lurched across the room toward the basement door. He made it, and putting a hand on the knob, guessed that he should try and head back toward his chair. The saw was still outside, however, and he thought that the fresh air would do him some good, so he headed down the steps gripping the handrail for all he was worth. He fell against the wall at the bottom, regardless. By the time that he got to the door onto the patio, where he stopped for a few seconds and leaned his head against the glass, the rain was falling in sheets. He opened the door and stood in the doorway. He closed his eyes and breathed in the fresh smelling cool air, hoping that it would clear his head, but when he opened them again he felt the ground rocking like the water, which rippled violently. He put his hands on the door facing, made a mental count to three, was sure to step over the boards of the floor frame he was building and started toward the saw that was still smeared with his own blood. All his will was put toward getting to that saw, and all his attention was directed toward it. That was why he didn't see the rake that he had left there after he had leveled the ground for the bonus room. His foot hit the head of it flush and the handle flew up and cracked him hard in the nose.

If anything good came from Daniel cutting his finger, it was the fact that it took his mind off the terrible headache that he had that morning. The rake, in turn, brought that headache back and for a few minutes took his mind off his finger, his wife and all of his other problems. It also knocked off the cobwebs that the painkillers had draped over his brain. He just stood there, thinking of nothing but his nose. Holding his nose, caressing his nose, cursing his nose, bleeding through his nose. He was so disoriented that he just kept going in the direction that he had been heading when the rake had hit him. He whacked into the rake again. This time the blow knocked him backward where he tripped over the floor frame and fell back against the basement door.

"Wow, I bet that hurt!" a voice said as he lay there watching dots change hue, turn into stars, back into dots and explode in huge splashes of color. "Hey, man, you okay?" Daniel's injured hand raised up in front of him, mostly by reflex, and he could feel it grasped by a firm callused hand which seemed to stay away from his hurt finger. He was pulled up right and another hand was laid across his shoulders. "Your nose is bleeding pretty good; you got a towel or something like that?"

"There's a bathroom in the basement. There should be a towel in there."

"Okay, I'll be right back." Daniel could feel the door press into his back as the stranger went into the basement and laid his chest onto his knees until he could feel the door and a hand on his back again. "Okay, put this on your nose and give it steady pressure." Daniel did as the stranger told him and within minutes the pain subsided and he first began to wonder who the person was who had been talking to him and taking care of him.

As Daniel was helped to his feet, he could smell the man before he could even see him and, as his vision slowly became clear, so did the figure that led him to one of the saw horses set against the back of the house. The man was on the short side, barely coming to Daniel's shoulders, and he looked like he smelled. He was disheveled and dirty-looking. He obviously hadn't had a bath in a week or two at least. His stringy black hair was wet and hung well past his shoulders, and he had a beard of similar appearance that reached his chest. He was wearing a pair of baggy cut-off khakis, sandals and a very dirty Rush t-shirt. He leaned Daniel back against one of the saw horses and smiled like he was seeking approval for something. He had a tooth missing a few left of the middle and the one beside it was a great deal darker than the rest. Daniel searched for something to say and, when he finally found something, his response was far from cordial.

"What are you doing here?" His companion responded immediately and didn't seem to be taken back at all.

"Getting dry."

"I mean what are you doing in my yard?" The man looked at him and gestured around him.

"Getting dry man; getting out of the rain."

"You make it a habit of hanging around in other people's back yards?"

"There was no fence, you don't have any signs posted or anything, but I'll leave if you want me to."

"No." Daniel was surprised to find that his response was almost as immediate as the stranger's had been, but he didn't want the man to leave. He had only been alone for a few hours but it was already too long so he guessed that if Saddam Hussein had been in his back yard he would have struck up a conversation. He did like this guy; he didn't know why but he liked something about the stranger's demeanor, he just couldn't put his finger on it. "You can hang around until the rain stops." The stranger smiled and nodded and they just leaned there and watched it rain for a good while, Daniel searching for something to say and the stranger simply smiling, like he just enjoyed being there. Daniel wondered if he was high on something.

"I've always loved the smell of rain," the stranger said. Daniel wasn't listening and was a little caught off guard, so he asked the man to repeat himself. "The rain, I've always liked the smell that a good rain brings with it."

"Oh." Daniel muttered and was pretty sure that the man was on something and that it was probably a hell of a lot stronger than Bud Light.

"It makes everything smell so clean, like it's washed away all the impurities and other garbage. Everything smells fresh."

"Maybe this is what it smelled like when the world was new, when everything started." Daniel was saying this mostly out of politeness, but he did take a deep breath and the air did smell pleasant. It made him a little less eager for the rain to stop. It calmed him down as well and he relaxed. Looking out across the lake he began watching the pattern of countless circles that took on a soothing rhythm as the rain lessened a little.

"Oh, it is." The stranger said and Daniel tensed up again and took a step away from him. The stranger just moved closer and Daniel began to notice the man's body odor again. "So what happened to your finger?" He asked and Daniel had to think for awhile before he remembered what the man was talking about.

"Oh, I cut it on that saw yonder." Absently Daniel held up his middle finger and showed it to his new friend.

"You got a license to fly that thing, Hoss?"

"Sorry." said Daniel when he realized that he was flipping off his new companion. "That's where I was heading when I hit that rake. I was coming to get the saw out of the rain."

"Need a hand getting it in?" Daniel looked out from beneath the deck and noticed that it had stopped raining.

"Uh, sure," and they both trotted out to the table saw and, grabbing each side, carried it back under the deck. Daniel took the towel that he had on his nose and started to wipe off the table saw. The stranger picked up a small backpack and a trash bag from around the eaves of the house and headed past the basement door. "You leaving?" Daniel asked, not really wanting the man to go but then again not wanting him to feel like he wanted him to stay.

"Yeah, the rain stopped. I want to get on the road and get to where I can get some more shelter before the bottom falls out again."

"Heading into town?"

"Yeah, I'm looking to finagle something to eat."

"Wait right here." Daniel told him and, throwing down his towel, rushed into the basement and up the stairs. He had brought home a large bucket of KFC the night before last with the hopes that Lisa would be home. There was plenty left and Daniel hated leftovers, so he grabbed the bucket out of the refrigerator and started downstairs. He didn't know why he was shelling out food to a bum that he didn't even know, but he practically ran downstairs and stopped in the basement as the rain began to fall again. He called out to the stranger to hold on a second and then went back up to the hall closet and rummaged through it until he found the Carolina Panthers raincoat that Lisa had given him for his previous birthday. It was what he had asked her for and, when he had gotten it he had chomped at the bit through a four-month drought until he would finally get to wear it. It hung way down past his waist, had a hood, and a zip out lining. He took it off the hanger, held it out in front of him and took one last look at it before he went back downstairs.

"Wow!" the man yelled and his face lit up like the Fourth of July. Then Daniel gave him the coat. "Man, this is something else. You sure you want to give me your coat? I haven't ever had anything this nice!"

"They stunk this year anyway." Daniel said, speaking of the Panthers. "I'm thinking about switching over to the Redskins anyway. Go ahead and take it."

"Man, this is nice!" The man set down his pack and the chicken and slid into the coat. Then he picked them back up.

"The lining zips out," Daniel said, already regretting his decision but determined to see it through.

"It feels warm, I'll keep it in." The man pulled the hood up and then zipped it as high as it would go so all that was visible of his face were his eyes, nose, his moustache, and a few wisps of grimy hair. "I better get going, but thanks again." He stuck out a hand and, in the second before grasping it Daniel could see a huge scab on the stranger's palm. The thought of pressing the man's flesh turned his stomach, but as soon as they linked paws, all his apprehensions vanished and the man's smiling eyes and honest gratitude brought a smile that had been gone since that morning when he woke.

"Be careful," Daniel said as the man released his hand, stepped gingerly over the rake and disappeared around the corner of the house.

IV
The Afganeranians

While Daniel had been trying hard to drive himself to the hospital and not bleed all over his truck while he was doing it, Tony Dorsett was parked at the curb along Depot Street, sitting on the tailgate of his truck smoking a cigarette. His son, T.J. was inside the Federal Building setting up a new computer network for the Department of Agriculture, which was the only Federal agency still left in the building, and closed on Saturday, but the Dorsetts had been given a key. The building also housed the 4-H, the Senior Adults Association, an insurance company and a dentist's office.

T.J. Dorsett is regarded by most who know him as at least borderline retarded in most cases except for his ability with anything mechanical. T.J. is a whiz with anything from a pocket watch to a car engine, to a computer. It's a proven fact around Welbourne County that T.J. Dorsett can make things of this nature do things that they wouldn't normally do. In addition to his extermination business, Tony and T.J. have a computer sales and service franchise that they run out of the backroom of Dorsett and Son Exterminators and Computer Sales and Repair. It was the only one of its kind in the county and had all the major contracts with businesses in the area, including local, state and federal government.

It took Tony a good twenty minutes to get his new CD out of one of those elaborate thief deterrent harnesses that K-Mart puts on them. It was by a new rap artist called Poppa Kapinu and, as Tony was sliding it into the walkman, he heard a strange, but familiar sounding voice coming from the direction of the sidewalk.

"'Scuse. Is Federal Building?" Tony looked up to see two of the easterners from the van leaning on the side of the truck, looking at him and smiling. Their teeth were so white that they looked like they had been painted on. "Is Federal Building?" one asked again. "We are looking for post office."

"That's the Federal Building, but the post office ain't in there; it's a couple of blocks over down at the end of First." Just as he had gotten the words out of his mouth, he realized who he was talking to and did a little mental butt kicking, his own that is.

"What is in Federal Building?" The other one asked as Tony got up and walked around to the side of the truck so he could get a better look at them. They were wearing brand new very clean creased blue jeans, new jogging shoes with the "N" on the sides and t-shirts. One said "Fender Guitars" and the other had a series of stick drawings on it. The captions under the drawings said, "I don't have a drinking problem: I drink. I get drunk. I fall down. No problem." They were also wearing identical hats, very cheap ball caps that said, "Eat more possum."

"No government agency in there except the Department of Agriculture." Tony didn't think that this would hurt, seeing as he had already blabbed everything else.

"Is Ag-Ag...."

"Agriculture, you know. Farming, farms."

"Ah." They both said and nodded in unison. "Thank you." Tony didn't respond but watched them as they walked to the sidewalk that led up to the building and stood staring. As they stood there, they put their arms around each other's waists and slipped a hand into the other's back pocket. They stood there and stared until T.J. exited the building, tool box in hand, and headed down the sidewalk toward them. They parted and nodded their heads. T.J. passed by them and never acknowledged their presence, which he does with pretty much everybody. As he reached his Daddy, Tony ripped the toolbox out of his hand, threw it into the back of the truck, ushered T.J. into the passenger side seat, and burned rubber all the way down Depot Street, past the two men as they strolled along arm in arm gesturing to the Federal Building over their shoulder and smiling broadly.

"Okay, go 'head." Purdie Mae Pearce called to Tony as she put the receiver back on its cradle, but, instead of walking to the counter where he was, she went into the back storeroom. Tony leaned back and blew a long puff of smoke toward the ceiling. Beside him T.J. ate his french fries, all the time staring down into the plastic basket which was lined with wax paper. When she finally came back to the counter, Purdie Mae plopped a large stack of Styrofoam to-go containers down onto the counter and began stacking them underneath it. After she was finished, she looked around the room to see if there was anything else that needed doing before she leaned one elbow on the counter in front of Tony. "I said I was listening."

"Yeah, you looked like you're hanging on my every word," Tony said, putting his cigarette out in a glob of ketchup.

"I was. You said that you saw a van fulla weird characters out on Adams Ford Road. So what?"

"It wasn't just a van fulla weird characters; it was a bunch o' Easterners."

A bunch a who?" asked Purdie Mae's friend, Rufus, who sat on the stool next to Tony, talking to them over a copy of *Riders of the Purple Sage,* his long chocolate-colored fingers stretching over the back to the point that they could almost lace together at the spine.

"Easterners....," Tony started to say.

"Kind of like that bunch that was in here last week." Purdie Mae pulled a tray of half full salt shakers out from under the counter and started refilling them. "Where was they from? Elizabeth City?"

"Rodanthe."

"Right, and that reminds me we need to head down to Manteo this week or next to that Christmas Store. I need to pick up some stuff 'fore...."

"No, no, no!" Tony wasn't sure if Rufus and Purdie Mae were kidding or not, but they were getting on his nerves and he almost forgot that he was scared of Purdie Mae. "They were Middle Easterners, Afganeranians. You know, some of them Muslims."

"So," said Purdie Mae, "it's a public road; they can go where they want to go."

"Yeah," answered Rufus, leafing to the back of the book to see how many more pages there were to go.

"Then I saw two of 'em downtown casing the Federal Building. You know, they could be terrorists just like they been talking about on the news. They were acting sneaky."

"Like how?"

"Well, they just looked like they were up to somethin'."

"Like how?"

"Oh, think about it," Tony said, swatting T.J.'s hand away as he was trying to point out a shape in his left-over grains of salt. "Bunch of Muslims all together 'round here and it isn't like we have a lot of those people come through here. Then they're asking about the Federal Building. They may be planning to blow it up or something."

"Why in the world would they want to blow up the Federal Building?" Purdie Mae slammed a lid down on one of the salt shakers and wrinkled up her nose like she smelled something. "They got something against Dr. Lindsey?"

"No, they're after landmarks, symbols of the American way of life, they want to bring this country to its knees."

"By blowing up our Federal Building?" Rufus closed his book and slapped it down on the counter in front of him. "Why would they come here anyway? Don't they usually pick a target in New York or Washington, some place like that?"

"I don't know why they're here. All I know is that they are here and I know what they're up to."

"Well I don't see how you do." Purdie Mae said, "and I got work to do." She had started putting the salt shakers back down underneath the counter when she heard the loading dock bell ring. "Uh huh, there's the bread truck. Hey, you," she called to a little long hair who was sitting in one of the front booths. "You wanna earn that chicken you eatin'?" The fella took off a very nice Carolina Panthers coat and, folding it under his arm, started after Purdie Mae. "You, too, Sugarbear." Purdie Mae called and Gene Pickard, who had been sitting in the booth with the hippie, struggled to his feet and waddled around the counter toward the storeroom. "You know, if the rest of you fellas helped too, we'd get this over faster. So why don't you move your butts? There's a free cobbler in it for you."

V
The Little General
Translated from Arabic

The previous evening Tater returned from checking the equipment in the van and walked into the motel room to a sight that made him want to draw blood. June Bug and Skillet were lying on the bed. They had put in yet another American quarter from their small reserves of capitalist money into the bed, causing it to vibrate. Not only were they shirking their duties and alerting the entire building as to their presence (the bed shook the very walls) but Tater caught sight of them holding hands. They unclenched and pretended to study their American phrase books when Tater walked in. Of the four that he had left in the room, only Bubba appeared to be earnestly working toward the task at hand. He sat on the floor with his long legs crossed at his body and his knees stuck up in the air like a grasshopper's. A bevy of maps as well as their itinerary were scattered around him and he appeared to be taking copious notes. The Koran sat open on the floor beside him and he had taken off the American baseball cap that they had bought in a store when they first entered the country. June Bug and Skillet were whispering and giggling behind their phrasebooks and Skeeter sat with his back to the foot of the bed watching a sinful American film on television. On the screen, at which Tater could not look at for even a second and had to close his eyes and say a silent prayer to Allah, an infidel American man was groping and being groped by two buxom blond women. They were all three naked and were straddling a large motorcycle.

"Disgraceful!*" Tater screamed and everyone snapped to attention like soldiers in Allah's army, as they were chosen to be. "We have not been in America a week and already you are adopting the infidel's sinful habits!" He stalked to the T.V. and switched it off. "We are not here to watch other people fornicate, nor are we here to submit to our own body's lusts! When I return, you will all be tested as to your responsibilities concerning our mission! I advise you to become familiar with the task at hand or you will face my wrath!" He stomped into the bathroom and had hardly closed the door when the electronic grind of the movie's music began creeping in underneath it. Although it was not a designated time of prayer, Tater knelt down and pressed his forehead to the foul smelling tile.

Born in Egypt as Abdullah Ahmed Mustafa Muhammed Akkbar El-Abin, Tater was a third cousin of the sixth wife of Osama Bin Ladin's brother-in-law and had served as a cook for the Mujahedeen during the Russian invasion of Afghanistan. After the war he had sought every opportunity to join the growing battle with the infidels. Over the next twenty years Tater had tried to join every training camp, and almost every faction in the Middle-East, but he was not welcomed by either one. Having partial access to information regarding the plans of most of these terror groups, he was resolute in joining the jihad against the West, but, in one way or another, he had been left out. He had been locked in a closet and left behind when the American Embassy in Tehran was taken in '79 and was left at the dock in both the attacks on the Achille Lauro and the U.S.S. Cole. He was commended for his dedication to Islam and to Allah, he was admired by some for his knowledge of his religion, his homeland, of the infidels and the tactics to be used against them. What worked against him, what kept him from being accepted within the factions, from being taken seriously and being included as a productive member of the Nation of Islam, was the fact that he was just over three feet tall. He never questioned Allah as to why he had given him such a lack of height, because there was a reason (he was sure of it) and Allah knew best, he would provide. Tater was tired, however, of being patted on the head, of the mocking smiles of the men and the laughing eyes of the women barely visible through their burkas and veils; he had always hated seeing women smile. All he wanted to do was to prove himself to all those people, all those men of importance, within the nations of Islam who thought him no more than a joke, who called him names, and said that he was good for no more than cooking cuscus. He had actually been sitting on a cot in a back room behind his uncle's restaurant in Syria staring at a sharp curved blade that he had been carrying in the waistband of his pants. He was wondering whether it would best serve Allah in slitting his own throat, when a man who claimed to be a close acquaintance to Osama Bin Laden himself asked for him and was brought into his little room. He was told that he was needed for a special mission, one that would take him not only to America but to the area that served as that infidel country's backbone, its foundation. He was told that the attack he would lead would be unusual in its execution and would strike the infidels where they were at their most sensitive. He was told to get together four people that he could trust and that he would be contacted in a week. In less than a year all were landing in Atlanta with a coded list of contacts and rendezvous points. They bought a van and headed north into North Carolina stopping when Tater felt that Allah wished them to stop. They came to this little infidel town, found this sinful motel and all took names that Tater thought would help them to blend in with the native populace. He only wished that the other members of his faction were as devout and as loyal to the cause as he was. They were all relatives, but other than Bubba who was zealous, and was very talented in his area, but stupid as well, they all seemed so easily corrupted by the seductive trappings of American debauchery.

After he was finished praying he rose onto his knees, cracking his head on the toilet bowl on the way up. He knelt there rubbing his crown, cursing and listening to sounds of stupidity and depravity, the sounds of that movie playing and somebody giggling, as well as Bubba practicing his southern American English:

"Hah Dee. Hah Dee. Ho Dee." Tater climbed up onto an ornate box that he carried with him to assist him with his handicap, and looked into the mirror for several minutes. He was still not used to seeing himself without a beard and running a hand across each cheek almost retched at the feel of it, smooth, soft like a woman's. He splashed water on his face and it felt so cold. He could not wait to get out of this evil country and back to civilization.

A loud thump on the other side of the wall tore him away from his thoughts and as the sound of June Bug and Skillet laughing and cooing dripped through the wall his hand went to the curved knife hidden in the back of his jeans underneath his shirttail. He didn't know which one of them he was going to use it on, June Bug, Skillet, Skeeter or it might be best for everyone if he just turned it on himself.

VI
The Hessian

Marilyn Misenheimer sat on the foot of the bed and pulled a scratchy, blue motel blanket tightly around her. She tilted her head first one way then the other all the time staring at the T.V. trying to figure out what the people on the screen were doing. The instructions that were bolted to the top of the T.V. said that they had an X rated movie service and her husband Mitchell had followed the instructions, but the people on the screen couldn't be having sex. There were three of them and they were on a motorcycle. It didn't look like how she remembered it. It looked like, well she didn't know what it looked like, but it wasn't anything that she wanted to watch.

She got up and staggered to the window all the time staring at her feet, watching them wobble back and forth on heels that were at least three inches high and felt no wider than the lead of a pencil. She pulled the tacky orange and burnt umber curtains across her, lest anybody outside see her, and stared not really through the window and into the parking lot, but rather at her reflection in the glass and that of the room behind her. The dozen candles that had been lit and sat around the room cast her mostly as a silhouette but she could still make out her face which had been done up with a thick layer of make-up that made her look slutty. She pulled the curtain and blanket out from her body and looked at what she was wearing; the dark red bodice, the garters, the fish net hose and the shoes which made her feet scream at her like they were breaking. The whole thing was embarrassing, it was degrading and it made her feel very uncomfortable, but it was all part of spicing things up like Mitchell and Dr. McCandless had told her.

Marilyn had always thought that they had a perfect marriage. Their twenty-first anniversary had been the February before. They had two children, a very nice house in the best neighborhood in town and they were well off. Marilyn remembered a great many arguments just after they had been married but they had dwindled in number. Yes they still had a spat or two every so often but Marilyn was always quick to let Mitchell win just like her mother had told her. They had it all or so she thought. It seemed that Mitchell didn't share her rosy view of the situation.

Throughout their marriage both Marilyn and Mitchell had their own projects but the last few years Mitchell's seemed to take more and more of his time. Between work, golf, bowling, town council, church and Rotary he was hardly ever home and when he was he mostly stayed in front of the T.V. or shut away in his study doing whatever. Since their first child Marshall had been born they had always promised themselves that at least one night would be family night. A night for them to put their other plans and activities on hold and spend a few uninterrupted hours together but eventually even family night fell by the wayside, gobbled up by time at the office and with Mitchell's buddies. When Marilyn confronted her husband about it he said that Marshall, their oldest, had left home and that their youngest son Martin wasn't interested. That he was at the age where he would rather spend time with himself or people his own age rather than plopped down on the couch with his folks watching *Steel Magnolias* or whatever movie that Marilyn chose to pick out for the evening. That simply wasn't true, Marilyn knew it wasn't. True, Martin never said that he wanted to have a night with his parents. He wouldn't come right out and express his feelings, he was like his father in that respect.

It was right about that time that Marilyn started looking for something to take up a little of her time. She had some of the work that she was doing at church, and the Literate Ladies Book Club but that still left a great deal of free time. She had home schooled Martin until the fourth grade and a rather ugly incident at the public library. Then Mitchell enrolled him in public school. Marilyn had to admit he was doing better but he preferred staying home with his mommy. He never said so but he did, Marilyn could tell. Then she joined the local chapter of the Daughters of the American Revolution, did all the paper work and traced her mother's family back to a Hessian who actually fought on the side of the British in the Revolutionary War. He was captured and fathered a girl with the young woman whose job it was to bring him food once a day. Technically since Marilyn's connection with the revolution was through an illegitimacy it should have been considered null where the D.A.R. is concerned, but she begged, bitched and cajoled until the main office in Washington D.C. approved it through a statement in a letter from the girl as she wrote back to her parents after the Hessian escaped, taking her with him. It read:

"I fear I shall be with this evil man until the end of my days." To all those other people who had been researching the same family this letter meant that the girl had been kidnapped and feared that either her life was not going to last very much longer or that she would spend the rest of that time lashed to the "evil" Hessian. In reality the girl was found several months later wandering in the woods. She was wearing the Hessian's boots and clucking like a chicken. Marilyn, however, claimed that the line out of the girl's letter actually read: "I've found that I shall be with this eloquent man to the end of my days." And that the girl's scrawl and the condition of the paper, which had obviously not been taking care off, had prevented the letter from being read clearly. Obviously this was a star-crossed romance and the lovers had escaped an oppressive society that sought to restrain true love. They rode off into the sunset and lived happily ever after, that is until a bout with fever led to the girl's unfortunate loss of her good sense. The Hessian was found and hanged a year later, according to Marilyn unjustly.

Marilyn showed up at her first meeting having just received notification from the national office in Washington that she had been accepted only to take part in the vote to disband the chapter immediately due to sagging interest. The vote was cast five for disbanding and one against, that being Marilyn who went on a personal campaign to contact the surviving members who were not able to attend the final meeting and try and talk them into voting against disbanding. She combed every rest home in Welbourne County and the surrounding area and was able to find only one more member who could hear what Marilyn was saying and had control of her faculties. That woman had been expelled from the charter for dumping a punch bowl over a fellow member's head after a heated debate over what year Lucius Welbourne's second to youngest daughter Bersistie was born. That woman chose to vote for disbanding as well making the final vote six for one against.

While she was doing her research for the D.A.R. Marilyn corresponded with the Welbourne County Historical Society and joined just before her fateful meeting with the Daughters. She had talked at great length with Dr. Francis Beck a local historian and a distant cousin on her husband's side. They met in the library shortly after the D.A.R. disbanded and Marilyn informed him of what happened and bared her soul about wanting something to fill her time, her interest in history and her difficulty in finding an outlet for her interests and her energy. Dr. Beck then encouraged her to let him nominate her for treasurer of the Historical Society. He told her that the office had been vacant since Tootie Watson was stabbed at the fall meeting. Marilyn jumped at the chance despite the danger to her well being and took to her post with all the vigor of Roosevelt charging up San Juan Hill. The next year Dr. Beck nominated her for president, a post which she received and took to even more enthusiastically than she had served as treasurer. Soon the Historical Society moved and acted like Hitler's S.S. and any threat to the preservation and study of the heritage of Welbourne County was met with a blitzkrieg style attack and soon it was said that if it looks old leave it where it is and put in an anonymous call to Marilyn Misenheimer. You'll live longer that way. In her year long tenure as the president of the Historical Society a heritage book was written and another planned. The Civil War memorial was refurbished and the confederate flag returned to it. This sparked a heated debate between the Historical Society and the local chapter of the N.A.A.C.P. which three times erupted into violence. As of today the flag still flies. In addition no less than six buildings within the county were slated to bear the designation of historical landmark. These were definitely her pet projects, spurred on by architectural expert Beck and the last of these projects was the previously mentioned Adam's Ford Toll Road House.

Marilyn's involvement in the Historical Society did give her the release she had wanted but it was also an indirect factor in putting her in a sleazy motel dressed like a much older dark headed Madonna. It filled her time so completely that when Mitchell Misenheimer came home late from one of his many endeavors his wife would not be there waiting up for him. She was either out on some mission for the Historical Society, engrossed in a phone call with Dr. Beck or one of her other cronies, deep in thought and as much company as a dead possum or, having finally run out of energy, dead asleep. This didn't set well with Mitchell. It was alright for his wife to wait around for him to decide to give her a little attention but when it was him sitting alone at night watching television or reading the paper when he had other things on his mind that wouldn't cut it. Then there was the fact that his wife seemed to ignore him totally while she was awake and was around. He would listen to her rant, whine and get misty eyed about all manner of historical and genealogical causes, facts and dates. He'd hear about the Hessian for at least an hour a day, and oh how he hated that damn Hessian. He never told his wife this but he was glad he was hung and he was just about to drive Mitchell crazy just like he had what's her face the illustrious ancestor of Marilyn's whom the Hessian had knocked up. Then it was time for Mitchell to tell about his day which would surely be interrupted two words into his sentence for Marilyn to start in again about some clap trap of a hotel that George Washington slept in, with somebody or other while he was president. He would end up just walking away while Marilyn was still talking, cracking open the paper or a Kinky Friedman novel along with a cold beer and dozing off in his easy chair. Marilyn seemed to lose her interest in movies, which they had always enjoyed as a couple years ago, that is movies that weren't about the Civil War. She didn't seem to care to leave the house when it wasn't on some errand for the Historical Society, even missing the annual Blackbriar Country Club Spring Fling, which she had always enjoyed before, to go crawl through some chigger infested graveyard.

The idea that all was not bliss in the Misenheimer's marriage finally found a crack through Marilyn's granite skull when she checked Mitchell's e-mail late one night while he was still out bowling. She had given her own email log-in and password to Imogene Archer for her to take care of some Historical Society business and then had come to words with Imogene over whether or not they should take up the cause to protect the old city jail. The jail had been vacant for going on twelve years due to asbestos, dry rot and an infestation of copperheads. Marilyn, of course, wanted to protect the building; Imogene thought it best if they let the building be leveled. Marilyn always claimed it was because Imogene's father had spent so much time there when he was alive.

Imogene had been using Marilyn's e-mail to send messages to other members of the society, confusing her own intentions with Marilyn's, so Marilyn had little choice but to use Mitchell's business e-mail. She had been checking and sending messages a little under a week when she checked the in-box and did not find any messages from Dr. Beck or anybody else from the society. What she found was a message from the mayor, Johnston Farley, who was a good friend of Mitchell's, so that wasn't unusual. What caught her attention was the subject line which read, "Gone fishing, caught two beauties!" The message drew her attention because neither the mayor nor Mitchell fished. She opened the file without a moment's hesitation: Her husband's privacy was never much of a priority to her. The message from the mayor told Mitchell that he had met two women somewhere or other who would meet them in Myrtle Beach during a little "golfing trip" that they had been planning over the last couple of months. The women had even agreed to share a couple of hotel rooms that they had arranged, and they might even cut the golf short and just hang around at the Farley's beach house in Garden City. Marilyn had initially slammed down the lid of the laptop but, not being able to walk away, she booted it back up again, read the rest of the message and then the entire thing over again. The one consolation was that the message ended in an encouraging, almost pleading way, like the mayor was trying to convince Mitchell to do all this, that he wasn't quite convinced. This is what kept her from throttling him the minute he came in the door. That kept her from saying anything at all, but acting normal as he drank a beer and went up to bed.

To Mitchell his wife acted a little too friendly. She didn't want to talk history, she never mentioned the Hessian, she only asked how his day had been, how bowling had gone and she had actually sat down and listened as he had told her. She never once opened her mouth until she told him good night and that she loved him before giving him a little peck on the lips and watching him disappear up the steps. The next morning they rose and had breakfast together, which again was unusual, and Mitchell left the house with the strong suspicion that something was rotten in Denmark and it wasn't the cheese. He had hardly gotten out the door when Marilyn was on the phone with Phoebe Farley, the mayor's wife and Marilyn's best friend until she was replaced by the Hessian and all the charms of historical preservation. Marilyn told Phoebe that she had to see her, despite the fact that Phoebe had plans that morning.

"Well, cancel," Marilyn told her. "It isn't like the book club will blow away on the wind. Some of those old biddies might, but the club will be there next month. We need to talk." As Pheobe dressed and headed toward the Colonial Diner, a little eatery that sat on the outskirts of the Blackbrair County Club and was run by the same management, she went over in her mind all the different ways that she could tell Marilyn Misenheimer to cram it. Their husbands had been friends since high school and after Marilyn had moved to Welbourne County and started dating Mitchell, Phoebe had started associating with her because Marilyn had no other friends in town. She did it as sort of a favor for Mitchell and Johnny but it didn't take her long to grow to like Marilyn and they were best friends from that point on, or at least until she joined the Historical Society. It was then that Pheobe would go a week or two without seeing Marilyn. Their phone calls, which usually ran an hour or two, were either reduced to a series of "yeah's" and "uh-huh's" on Marilyn's account or an hour long treatise on local history when it was Pheobe's turn to do the "yeah's" and "uh-huh's". Now it was put all your plans aside and meet me for brunch.

Marilyn had always been full of herself and abrupt often times to the point of rudeness, but here lately she had been down right ridiculous. When they had been friends, Pheobe had overlooked an awful lot. There had been a lot of snotty comments, a lot of afternoons tagging along behind the Divine Miss M like a poodle while she conducted her own business, and a lot more that would take several books the size of *War and Peace* to list. No, Miss. M was going to get an earful this morning and it wasn't until Phoebe walked into the Colonial and saw the sad almost grievous look on Marilyn's face that she cooled off and slid into the chair across from her.

The thing that always bothered Marilyn more than anything when she told her best friend that her husband was cheating on her was that Phoebe never acted surprised. Sure, it had happened before. Phoebe had caught Johnny having an affair with a twenty-year old sales clerk from the Teen Haven Boutique and had even left the mayor and lived with her daughter in Arizona for a little while, but she came back. Marilyn never knew why she came back and she never knew what happened after Phoebe left the Colonial that morning.

Marilyn brought it all up to Mitchell when he got in at one the next morning and followed it with one simple question, "Why?" He never really answered her until the next morning and his answer was much the same as her complaint with her husband before she had joined the Historical Society: That he was just tired of sitting at home alone; that sometimes he didn't feel that anybody even noticed when he got home, that it was more like having a roommate than a wife. Marilyn told him that she understood and asked, begged pleaded with him not to give up on them yet. He denied vehemently that he had ever "given up", and they both planned to get some help.

They both cleared their schedules for the same times over the next four months for appointments with Dr. McCandless, a marriage counselor that the mayor had suggested, and Marilyn actually found herself looking forward to the first session. When the time rolled around, she and Mitchell drove into Winston-Salem and spent a good hour bearing their souls, listing their grievances and telling each other what they wanted out of their marriage. Two weeks after that first session, Marilyn found herself sitting on a threadbare mattress in a sleazy motel watching three people defy gravity on the back of a motorcycle. Dr. McCandless had informed Mrs. Misenheimer that sexual intimacy could increase the bond between them and reduce stress for them both, as well as boost Marilyn's immune system, tone her pelvic muscles and flush wastes products from her body, that they should put aside a few nights toward fulfilling each others needs and fantasies. Marilyn couldn't say that she had any fantasies, but it was Mitchell who had dreamed up their present scenario, in order to save their marriage.

Marilyn backed away from the window when she heard a door open one room over. She watched the T.V. for a little while. One woman had left and the remaining one along with the man had moved onto a bear skin rug. Marilyn listened intently toward the bathroom door; the shower had shut off minutes before and Mitchell had called: "I'll be right out don't start without me!" Marilyn rolled her eyes and adjusted her thong, but didn't answer because her attention was pulled back to the window by a man shouting. He wasn't speaking English and his language was so garbled and alien-sounding that she slipped back to the window and parted the curtains just a touch so that she could see into the parking lot. A very, very short, dark-skinned man stood over another who had spread a small rug down into one of the parking spaces directly in front of the window. He was admonishing the second man and attempting to yank him to his feet by the back of his collar, but his lack of height made it impossible. The whole scene would have been comical had it not been so shocking and out of place. The second man got to his feet and scurried off and Marilyn could hear the door open and shut again. The short man went around to the back of a rusty, orange van in the next parking space, and, glancing around the parking lot, opened the back door and threw the rug in. In the second that the door was open, Marilyn could see all sorts of crates and equipment, including what looked like a rifle, not a hunting rifle, but the one she always saw people who looked a lot like this man firing at some unseen enemy on CNN. There were also a lot of long wooden cases, the kind that she knew the military transported ammunition in. Her son Marshall had made stereo speakers out of two similar boxes.

The man looked toward her and she backed up quickly, hitting the backs of her legs on the bed. She sat down onto it with a creak, then froze and stared through the part in the curtain, holding her breath lest she see the short Eastern man's burning dark eyes glaring in at her. She was afraid to move, afraid to breathe. He might hear her; even her heart beating and the running water in the bathroom sounded way too loud. She sat there and prayed until she heard the door next door shut again. A second later the whole affair was punctuated with the bathroom door opening and Mitchell's voice called to her, "Okay Mommy. Ready or not here I come!"

VII
Whitewashed Tombs

When Daniel woke up the morning after the stranger's visit, he felt like a million bucks. For one thing, he wasn't hung over. He had watched it rain for a little while after the stranger had left and, when he had gone upstairs, he went straight for the open case on the kitchen counter. He had cracked open a can, took a swig and almost gagged. It was water. He took another drink to make sure, and that's what it was, water. The coldest, cleanest freshest tasting spring water that he had ever poured into his mouth. He actually finished the can and then opened another again expecting beer and getting the same good-tasting water. He stared into the can between swigs, dumfounded, wondering how this could happen. He had gotten beers that were weak or had water in them, but never pure water like this. Was this normal? Did they mix up the cans at the store or the brewery? Daniel shrugged it off and made a mental note to go down to the Stop and Rob a little later and buy more beer, and he spent the rest of the night eating frozen pizza, drinking the water and watching a *Kolchak: The Night Stalker* marathon on the Sci-Fi channel. He went to bed early for him, 10:30, and slept like a log.

When Daniel woke up, he felt, physically and mentally refreshed, like he could take on the world. He flipped through the channels looking for some cartoons and dialed Lisa's cell phone number. He got her voice mail, James Earl Jones again, and hung up. He sat there for awhile watching Wile E. chase the Road Runner when the sound of bells came drifting across the water from the little Pentecostal church across the lake. Daniel could see the church through the sliding glass door and the scene looked like something out of a Thomas Kinkaid painting with the church's white steeple jutting out of a grove of trees colored a bright green and sparkling with the light of a new day. Daniel always thought that the little white church looked a little out of place in and among the new houses, manicured lawns and lighted sidewalks of the Oakton Estates. He wasn't the only one. He and Lisa had moved in among a firefight between the builders who had just about gotten the church's deacons to agree to sell and the Welbourne County Historical Society. The Historical Society, headed by Marilyn Misenheimer, whose husband Mitchell bowled on the same team with Daniel, had claimed that an important patriot had been wounded in the woods nearby during a Revolutionary War skirmish and that he had been brought to that same little church, been treated, and born again just a few minutes before he had died. For that reason Marilyn said that the church was a historical landmark which forbad its being demolished. Daniel and Lisa had not even moved in before they got visits from, first, the builders and, second, Marilyn, both of whom gave their perspective points of view. He and Lisa had both signed Marilyn's petition; Lisa didn't care either way and they both wanted to support the Misenheimers, so the church ended up staying. Daniel never said it out loud, but he kind of liked the little church. He liked how it looked from his window as he watched it across the water and when he was up at that time on Sunday morning, which wasn't often, he liked listening to the bells.

That morning their mellow tones floating toward him on the wind put a strange thought in his head. He decided that he would go to church. He hadn't been in well over a year and, for some reason, the thought didn't cause his eyes to glaze over the way it usually did. He bounded out of his chair and looked over his shoulder toward the little white steeple as he trotted into the bedroom.

He never planned on going to the little white church, although he definitely drew his inspiration from it. It was one of those praise, glory and hallelujah Pentecostal churches, where people yelled and spoke in tongues, had visions, that sort of thing, and that was definitely not Daniel's thing. He showered, shaved, changed the dressing on his finger and put on the dark blue suit that Lisa had bought him a year or two before, the one he had worn only three times since. It made him think of his wife again and he started to call her, but he figured he'd get nothing but the same recorded message and he didn't want it to ruin his good mood. He also thought of the raincoat that he had given the stranger the day before as he put on his suit coat and began slipping things-keys, change, wallet, cell phone-into his pockets. He had the same brief pang of regret for having given his coat away but it didn't last long. If Lisa had a problem with it, then she should have been there. At that moment just wearing something that his wife had given him rubbed him the wrong way and he debated taking the suit off and changing clothes, but a glance at his watch told him that there wasn't much time to get there before the 11:00 service. So he straightened his tie and headed out.

Daniel never considered himself a church goer, but he was at least moderately religious. He had always believed in God, he never doubted that he existed and he did talk to him occasionally, mostly asking for something or other or promising not to drink again; the later was most frequently done while kneeling over the toilet. His family had gone to church off and on when he was a kid. There was a Quaker Meeting a few miles from his house and they would attend there for a month or two until his parents got bored with it or his father got mad at somebody. Then they would go for six or so months and not attend until one of his parents had some kind of epiphany or got religion for some reason and they would go for a month or two and then quit again. They did always attend at Christmas and Easter. Reverend Hartsoe from Central Methodist Church had come to see Daniel and Lisa right after they had gotten married and they had attended for a little while. Wade, the Mayor and the Misenheimers went there so it had that attraction, but the apple didn't fall too far from the tree and Daniel started sleeping in on Sunday mornings and letting Lisa go without him. Then she stopped going as well.

Daniel got to Central Methodist just as the service was starting, slipped in the door and took a spot on the back pew on the aisle right beside a pretty little woman trying and failing to restrain a squirming toddler. He really wanted to get in, hear the service and get out without anyone he knew seeing him, but while the plate was being passed, he had been desperately fishing through his wallet for something less than a twenty. He looked up to see the mayor holding the plate down for him, smiling ear to ear.

"Hey, bud, what's going on?" he whispered as Daniel dropped in a five. The mayor motioned for Daniel to meet him outside after the service. Daniel nodded and sat back, almost mad that he had been discovered, but the Mayor looked so glad to see him he let it go and settled in to listen to the sermon.

Hartsoe started by making a connection between his sermon and *Indiana Jones and The Last Crusade,* which was on AMC the week before. Daniel had been sure to catch it. He made reference to the scene at the end where Indy is forced to go through a series of tests to get to the Holy Grail, which was the only way to save his father.

"With Indy leading the way," Hartsoe went on, leaning over

the pulpit, the lights coming up underneath his chin giving his face an unearthly look to it. "they all made it to the last chamber which was guarded by a knight who had been kept alive by the power of the Grail for over a thousand years. Dozens of different cups in various sizes and shapes had been placed about the chamber: some are elaborate, gold vessels encrusted with gems, others are more plain and unassuming in appearance. The knight tells the men that they must choose, that the true Grail will give life, but all of the other false Grails will take life away. One of the bad guys went first and, taking a cue from a moll who was there with them, picked a gaudy, gold chalice. He dipped it into a vessel of water and took a drink." The preacher paused with his hands up under his chin like he was drinking from a cup. "There were a few seconds pause for dramatic effect and the man died, shriveling up and crumbling to dust before our very eyes. Then it was Indiana Jones' turn. He looked through all the cups and goblets that were there, he perused them for a moment." Hartsoe looked around on the pulpit like he was picking a cup himself. "And, spurred on by his father's screams of pain coming from the other chamber, picked a simple drab, dusty cup from somewhere near the back. 'This is a cup of a carpenter.' he said. 'You have chosen wisely,' the knight overseeing the selections said."

The sermon went on from there and it concerned the fact that Jesus was a simple man, he was not an aristocrat, he didn't have flashy suits, Rolex watches or SUV's. He was a simple carpenter and he led a simple life. The preacher made references to the big nice cars that were sitting about the parking lot and wondered if they were really necessary to just get around town and make a living. This would've given Daniel a little pang of guilt, but he remembered that the preacher himself drove a Cadillac so it didn't bother him too much. "He told us that we could find him among the poor and the outcast. He won't be at Blackbriar Country Club, friends," Hartsoe said closer to the end of his sermon. "He may be among those people whom we don't see as pretty, who don't have the wealth and affluence that we ourselves enjoy. In fact, during his lifetime Jesus did not spend a lot of time around the rich and the powerful. He was very critical of those in power, calling the Pharisees who were the among the most powerful, 'white washed tombs.' What he means by 'whitewash tombs,' my friends, is that they were pretty and attractive on the outside but dead and rotten on the inside. When he walked among us, he was a drifter, a vagabond with very little but the clothes on his back . We may have to go looking for Jesus, and who knows what kind of people we might have to associate with to find him. He doesn't like pretension. Remember his words about the Pharisees. He didn't associate with them; he associated with the sinners. He may not tool down Wells Creek Boulevard in a Mercedes. We may find him in and among the flop houses and the homeless."

Reverend Hartsoe picked Daniel out of the congregation as he and his wife Fanny made their way down the aisle during the closing hymn. The preacher with his red face and perpetual grin which shows off a set of very white, obviously capped teeth. He passed by Daniel and squeezed his arm on the way by as Daniel pretended to sing *The Old Rugged Cross*. When Daniel met Hartsoe again, shaking everyone's hand on the way out. The minister gripped his hand hard enough to break it and pulled him close, putting the other hand on his shoulder.

"Well you are a sight for sore eyes! I am glad you came today! Fanny, look who's here. You remember Daniel!"

"Yes, welcome!" Fanny is a tall woman with a mouth so big that Daniel always wanted to look for a hook. She spread the corners of that mouth and showed off a set of pearly whites of her own. "Hope to see you back with us next week."

Daniel went outside and waited at the bottom of the steps. The day had turned off perfect. The Bradford pears were in bloom and a steady breeze blew the blossoms around all the exiting parishioners like feathers. The entire scene looked and felt so idyllic, save the strong smell that those trees always seem to exude, that Daniel just stood there loving life until a rough hand clutched him by one shoulder.

"Long time no see, fella." It was Mayor Farley and he had that same stupid grin on his face like somebody who was actually glad to see Daniel McDaniel. "Good to see you. Where's the wife?"

"Out of town on business again." Daniel placed a little extra emphasis on the again but it was lost on the mayor.

"Oh so you don't have to get back for anything. Why don't you run over to the Outback with us?" The mayor's wife, Phoebe, had walked up and smiled to Daniel over her husband's shoulder.

"Yeah, sure," Daniel said. "That'd be good."

"Cool," The mayor grinned. "I think Wade and Jane are going to tag along too." Daniel glanced toward the church entrance just as Wade Burgess, his wife Jane in tow, burst down the steps, muscled himself past two old ladies, and glanced toward the Mayor and Daniel. The Mayor gestured toward Daniel, and Wade gave a half-hearted wave and a nod and headed the other way. Daniel regretted agreeing to go. He hadn't counted on dealing with Wade today, and he dreaded having to sit down to dinner with him, but he had already agreed and he said that he would follow the Mayor. As he turned to head back to his truck, Pheobe called him back. "Before I forget, I wanted to ask about your finger."

Daniel told her that his finger was fine out of habit, but as he got into his truck, he was shocked that he had forgotten totally about his injury. He had changed the dressing that morning but he hadn't really thought about it. He hadn't taken any of the painkillers that his doctor had prescribed, but it felt fine; there was no pain at all. He backed out in front of Wade, who uncharacteristically held back and then waved him in like he was annoyed by the whole thing.

As he sat in the line of traffic behind the mayor, he poked the end of his injured finger against the steering wheel, wincing prematurely, but studying it like a monkey at a typewriter as he received no pain. He began jabbing the steering wheel and dash, harder each time, as he and the mayor inched toward the exit to the parking lot. He pulled his attention back to the task at hand as the mayor pulled out onto Church Street and he looked up to check traffic before pulling out himself. He found that his view toward the eastbound lane where the mayor was now turning onto First was blocked by the same stranger who had visited him at his house the day before. The man was no cleaner than he was the day before and he was holding a sign that said, "Hungry Pleeze Give." As Daniel drew even with him, the stranger smiled, waved and tugged on the lapel on the Carolina Panthers coat that Daniel had given him and which he was still wearing. The two locked eyes and, even after the stranger looked away and began gazing down past the line of cars behind him, Daniel froze where he was: surprised, shocked, embarrassed that somebody he semi-knew would be panhandling and out in front of a church at that. Most of all, he was torn over whether he should just go on, pretend that he didn't know the man, or give him a ride and get him out of there. He was still debating the point when he heard the familiar roar of Wade Burgess as he stomped past Daniel's passenger side window and stormed toward the stranger. Daniel hit the gas, squalling tires and flying down the street so he could catch up with the mayor and avoid seeing Wade tear into the little man wearing his jacket.

The Burgess' ended up beating Daniel to the Outback and, as Daniel walked up to where they were waiting for a table, Wade was bragging about his confrontation with the panhandler.

"Yeah, I got in his face. I told him to go beg somewhere else! Imagine begging for money in front of a damn church! I told him that I'd beat some of the scum off him, throw him off the property and then call the police."

"What about what Rev. Hartsoe said this morning. About looking for Christ among...." Daniel had wanted to say the same thing but hadn't had the nerve. He was glad Jane did.

"Oh that wasn't what he was talking about at all!" Wade bellowed, drawing all matter of glances from everyone in the restaurant. "That was a long time ago. The beggars these days are different. They beg because they're too lazy to go out a get a job. The ones they had didn't go around begging for money at churches!"

VIII
The Loading Dock Bunch

All of the regulars at Purdie Mae's Poultry Palace spent a relaxing weekend to themselves until early Sunday evening when the Poultry Palace's proprietor called each one and ordered them there first thing Monday morning. Purdie Mae had a huge shipment of chicken coming in, big because the distributor would be out of town the next month so she was getting two months at once. Purdie Mae never hired anybody other than herself, Rufus, who worked there when he wasn't at his other job fixing looms at Misenheimer Textile Mill, and Gene. She called on her regulars when there was extra work to the done. Why pay somebody when you could just cook up a mess of French fries and pay your help that way?

Just after 8 a.m., the Dorsetts, Gene Pickard and his new best friend, Stanley Fisher, as well as the bum who had been hanging around the place for a few days, as well as Purdie Mae were hanging around the loading dock. Rufus was somehow exempt and was allowed to go to work. Stanley and Gene were pitching pennies up against one wall; the stranger was standing behind them smiling at nothing in particular and the Dorsetts, well Tony anyway, was bitching about getting to work on time. These words were met with much harsher ones, as well as a goodly amount of threats, from Purdie Mae who told them to cool their jets until the truck got there and then they could go. As they fussed Gene, glanced over his shoulder, glad that Purdie Mae hadn't started griping at him again and praying that she didn't start anytime soon.

It hadn't been too long ago that Gene had been banned from Purdie Mae's Poultry Palace and from the company of Purdie Mae herself. Gene had worked at the Dog and Shake, which was the most popular restaurant in the county, a historical landmark according to Marilyn Misenheimer, and Purdie Mae's biggest competitor. That all put Gene on thin ice with Purdie Mae, but ever since he pinched her butt at the annual Poultry Palace Christmas party shortly after the bombing of Libya Gene had been told to stay away from Purdie

Mae, her restaurant and her associates under threat of torture and/ or death. For years that had been okay with Gene. He had never liked Purdie Mae. To tell the truth, she scared him to death; such was the case with almost everybody who met her, but Gene never told anybody; such was the case with every man who associated with Purdie Mae. He liked the food at the Dog and Shake better and, when he got a job there and started getting his meals free, he never had any need to go anywhere else. His best friend, Slobber McAllister, was still in Purdie Mae's good graces, most of the time, and he split his time between Gene and the rest of the bunch. Slobber would eat breakfast with Gene at the D & S and then eat dinner with Purdie Mae's crowd at the Poultry Palace. Gene and Slobber would hang out part of the time and then Slobber would go with Purdie Mae and them when Gene was busy elsewhere, like his quilting classes or Friday night bingo with Mama. Then it all changed. Gene always hated change and this time it was no different, everything seemed to fall apart.

First, Slobber was killed at a rally for Purdie Mae when she was running for mayor. To a lot of people in town, which in Gene's opinion included Purdie Mae, to lose Slobber was to lose a favorite pet, someone to laugh at. For Gene it was devastating. Slobber was his best friend, whom Gene considered more like a brother although Mama always called him a freak of nature. He was the only one who treated Gene like a grown man and talked to him like he was an equal, a partner, a buddy. Without Slobber, Gene's life was lonely and it was boring. There was life at home with Mama; there was work at the D & S and that was about it. He didn't know it until he was gone but Slobber had given his friend a reason to get out of bed. He had made life worth living. Gene missed Slobber now that he was gone; and he had loved him while he was alive, although he never did tell him or anybody else for that matter. Rumors that Gene was queer were so ingrained in the society of Ashewood Falls that they would probably outlive him.

Things got even worse a good three months after Slobber's death. One morning while Gene was busing tables, Wade Burgess, the county manager, whom, in addition to Purdie Mae, Gene avoided, came in along with Daniel McDaniel and sat down at a booth not far from where Gene was working.

"Hey, Tiny!" Wade called. He always called Gene that when he came into the restaurant. If it was out on the street and nobody could hear him, it would be something to the effect of "bushel britches" or "lard butt" and accompanied by an order to spend a few hours on a stair master. "I want to get some coffee and toast while I'm picking my slop here. Why don't you waddle on over to the counter and get me some coffee and..." He turned to Daniel. "What do you want, Danny Boy? Oh, don't worry about it. It's what he's here for..... And some orange juice." Gene wiped his eyes on his sleeve. He had been thinking about Slobber all morning, ever since watching *Texas Chainsaw Massacre* the night before. Slobber had loved horror movies and always made Gene watch them with him. Gene hated them but he had watched anyway.

Gene squeezed his considerable bulk between the tables and chairs, went behind the counter and brought Wade and Daniel coffee and juice, spilling both, and toast, remembering the butter but forgetting a plate. He laid the toast directly on the table.

"Hey, Einstein!" Wade called to him and, taking hold of Gene's arm, jerked him back to their table. "I don't think that there's a table in this place that I'd eat off of without at least a plate between it and the food. How about a plate for my bread?" Gene went back into the kitchen and didn't find any of the small plates that they served toast on. In reality they were sitting beside the sink on the drainer, but Gene, being a little on the stupid side anyway and distracted by thoughts of his dead friend and a growing irritation at Wade, didn't see them.

"Here, you go try this." Gene said as he shuffled back up to Daniel and Wade's table and took a napkin from the dispenser between them. He took the napkin and spread it out neatly on the table. The coffee that had been spilled there immediately began to bleed through it. Gene stacked Wade's toast in an orderly fashion on top of it. "There, that looks all right."

"Oh, wow, this is classy!" Wade said sarcastically. "Hey, fat boy, where am I supposed to stick my butter?

Gene supposed that Mike, his boss, had to fire him, but that took whatever wind Gene still had in his sails right out of them. Now he was reduced to spending morning, noon and night with Mama. Now, he loves Mama; he tells her that every day, but after a week or two she really started to drive him crazy and he started looking for any reason to get out of the house. One morning he was walking down Patton Avenue and the sight of Purdie Mae Pearce caught his attention. He was so deep in thought that he had wandered dangerously close to Purdie Mae's Poultry Palace and Rachet Jaws herself was standing in the front window looking at him. She held a thin piece of cardboard in her hand and she was gesturing for him to come inside. He never knew why he went inside. She wasn't using the finger that she normally did when she was gesturing to him, and she didn't look quite as menacing as she normally did, which was still enough to make a freight train take a dirt road, but he went inside and stood before her, wringing his 1998 North Carolina State quilting bee baseball cap in both hands.

"I got some tables that need busing."

"Uh.....," was all that Gene could say, wondering what this all had to do with him.

"You need a job, don't cha?"

"Uh....yeah."

"Well, get to busing these tables." Gene did as he was told and worked until five when he expected her to renege on her offer and send him home, none the richer. After he had swept and mopped the floor, however, drained and cleaned the fryers and refilled all the salt shakers, ketchup and napkin dispensers, she gave him a bag of chicken fingers and French fries that were left over and told him to come back at six the next morning. He still thought she was yanking his chain until six when she unlocked the door and let him in, showed him which locker in the storeroom was his, told him to get himself a cup of coffee and presented him with a couple of tax papers to sign.

The last few months had been far from ideal. Things at the Poultry Palace weren't as calm and quiet as at the D & S but they were all right. Gene had started hanging out with Stanley Fisher, who started coming into the Poultry Palace at about the same time that Gene had started working there. Stanley was an okay fella, but he was no Slobber. He wasn't as much fun as Slobber had been; in fact, Gene actually saw himself as the extravert in this relationship. After years with Slobber the notion had been as alien as working for Purdie Mae, but he had to adapt on both fronts. The strange thing was that working at the Poultry Palace proved to be a lot easier to get used to than Stanley Fisher. Again Stanley was a nice guy, Gene never doubted that, but it was Stanley's conspiracy rhetoric that got on Gene's nerves. Stanley was always saying that they were being watched or that he thought he was being followed, and no matter where their conversation went-from Disney Land to Mama canning green beans-there was a government conspiracy behind it and it was meant to erode the civil liberties of the citizens of these United States. According to Stanley, he had lived for awhile in Montana, after being born in Salisbury, and had moved back when some men that he worked with on a ranch convinced him that a black van they always saw sitting across the road from their driveway was the N.S.A. and that they were after them because of a connection to Ted Kaczinsky. In reality, the van was a police vehicle and they were after someone in the bunkhouse next to them for the manufacture and sale of mescaline, a fact that Stanley never knew and that his ex-bunkmates never told him.

As the crew waited for the chicken truck and Gene emptied his pockets of every last piece of change, Stanley proceeded to tell them all about an article that he had read on the internet about a secret society at Yale University. The members of that organization, according to Stanley, were among some of the most powerful men in history, men who have held incredible power over the lives of ordinary Americans.

"They say that both Bush's are in this society. So, right now our country's being controlled by 'em."

"Well," said Gene, pitching another penny toward the wall, "if Bush Sr. was a member and nothing happened when he was President we don't gotta worry about anything now."

"The Gulf War happened."

"Well, we won that one remember."

"Supposedly, but we don't know what the C.I.A. was really after."

"What was that?"

"Saddam's secret humus recipe," Purdie Mae muttered from where she paced the asphalt in front of the loading dock. Stanley was starting to tell them about the Knights Templar, an ancient secret society linked with the present day Masons, and those two organizations' role in creating the New World Order when the swish sound of tires on the wet pavement turned their attention to the Main Street entrance to the alley and they looked up expecting to see the much awaited truck there to deliver Purdie Mae's chicken. What they saw was a rusty, orange-colored van easing up the alley toward them.

"Oh, man!" Tony yelled, sliding off the loading dock to stand beside Purdie Mae. "It's them!"

"Who?"

"Them terrorists I was telling you about! The Afganiranians!"

"Oh, are you going on about that again?" Purdie Mae hissed as she slid up to sit on the loading dock and began lighting a cigarette.

Beside her T.J. was sitting Indian style and looking down at a small crack in the concrete. In his mind he was making his way down that crack in an inflatable raft.

"Going on about it nothing!" Tony quieted down as the van stopped across the courtyard at the loading dock behind Brown Home and Hardware. As they all looked four men got out and they did have the Arabian look of someone the crew on the loading dock had been no closer to than CNN. The youngest came around from the passenger side of the vehicle and helped the driver down from his seat. The driver barely cleared the van's headlights, but he was undeniably the leader of the group.

"Well, ain't he cute," said Purdie Mae in a cooing type of voice. "I could just pick him up and squeeze him."

"And he would probably just as soon slit your throat as look at you," said Stanley, creeping up behind her and kneeling down to look over her shoulder. "You know, Tony, I think you might be right about all this."

"Course I'm right."

"You know, they might be hooked up with that bunch in Afghanistan that Dubya got to bomb the World Trade Center."

"The President didn't get those guys to attack the World Trade Center! Gosh!"

"He's been awfully popular since then, hasn't he? What you think about that?"

"I think that you're stupid," said Purdie Mae waving a hand over her shoulder. "And I'm gonna box your jaws if you don't quit breathing on the back of my neck." They were all quiet, engrossed in the actions of the five men who seemed somewhat unnerved by the crowd who made their interest no secret as they stared, mouths agape, at every move the men made, save T.J. who was navigating a particularly treacherous bend around a dead ant. The little man barked out an order and one of the others bounded up onto Brown's loading dock and hit the big red button on the wall that rang the bell inside. As he came back down, the men huddled together and the short one began chattering loudly in a language that none of the gawkers on the loading dock could make head or tail of.

"We better be careful," whispered Stanley. "They might have a gun or knife, maybe a bomb. They might try and throw some anthrax on us."

"Shhh!" They watched the door on the loading dock open and Leonard Brown, the proprietor of Brown Home and Hardware, step out and walk down the steps from the loading dock to where the men were standing. Mr. Brown was a tall, red-headed man with a freckled face and a huge toothy grin with a part in the middle. As he took the short man's hand. Mr. Brown gave him that grin as he had done every other customer who had come through his door over the past twenty-seven years. The loading dock crowd watched as the men talked for a little bit and then Brown led the man up onto the loading dock and stood aside as he went in the rear entrance of his store. Looking over his shoulder Brown saw that he was being watched and, throwing up his hand, he flashed the bunch on Purdie Mae's loading dock his famous smile.

"Hey, Purdie Mae!"

"Hey, Good Lookin," Purdie Mae called back. "Workin' hard?"

"Hardly workin! Hey, how ya doin', fellas?"

"Fine."

"Fine."

"Fine." They watched all the men disappear inside and then Tony turned and asked the question had been burning on his tongue, "What do you think they want at Brown's?" Everybody sat silent for a moment, except for Purdie Mae who mumbled something about doing something to the chicken man.

"You know, I'll bet they're trying to buy a large amount of fertilizer," said Stanley. "A lot of it so's they can mix it with gas and make a bomb like that guy the government got to blow up that federal building in Nebraska."

"What!" snapped Tony and shot a look at Stanley that could have burned through a brick wall. "First off, it was in Oklahoma, the Oklahoma City Federal Building and the government didn't have anything to do with it!"

"You don't know that," Stanley shot back. "I seen on the internet......"

"It don't matter none either way," interrupted Purdie Mae. "Leonard don't have fertilizer. We checked on it last summer. You got to go out to K-Mart or over to the Feed and Seed."

"Lowe's in Salisbury might have some," said Gene from where he stood against the wall beside the stranger.

"They might." Purdie Mae turned to Gene and nodded in the affirmative.

"That don't matter; they might be gonna buy something else in there. You know, I heard that F.B.I. agents are trained to make a truth serum out of moth balls, prophylactic and shellac."

"Idiot." Tony started rubbing his forehead and fishing in his pocket for a B.C.

"What's a prophylactic?" Gene asked, walking out to the edge of the loading dock.

"It's what you put on your......"

"Hey, hush ya'll. They're coming out." Tony leaned up against the loading dock and tried to take his headache powder and act nonchalant at the same time. The result was a horrible face and a shower of headache powder and Mountain Dew flying all over T.J., who never moved. At the moment he had reached his rafting destination and was sharing a tent with the Dixie Chicks. The rest of the crowd simply looked and gawked as they had before. Mr. Brown shot them another smile and the five men, two of whom were carrying a large box, looked uncomfortable and made it a point not to look their way. "Man, I would give anything to find out what is in that box." Tony whispered and turned toward the rest of the crowd. They watched as the men got the box down onto the pavement and set it down. As they took a breather, they turned around with their backs to them. "Anything," Tony said again, more to himself than anybody.

"Okay," the stranger said and, jumping down off the loading dock, began walking toward the five men who were struggling to pick the box up again. The loading dock bunch had forgotten the stranger was there and stared in shock as he walked right up to the short man and slapped him on the back. "Hey, how ya'll doing. You know, you look like you could use some help!"

"Well, that's nice," Mr. Brown said; all the other men could do was look uncomfortable. The stranger grabbed one corner from the short man and began dragging the box toward the back of the van even before the other men had picked up their corners.

"Here you go, big'un. Let me help you here." The small man's demeanor went from being uncomfortable to being downright mad at being called "Bigun." The stranger helped get the box into the van and then stood there breathing heavily, his hands on his hips. "Wow, is that all?"

"No," said Brown. "They've got a pole in here to get."

"A pole? What is this thing?" The small man opened his mouth to say something but Brown spoke first.

"A basketball goal."

"Really?"

"Yep, these boys are a basketball team."

"Yeah."

"Yeah the Yeman Olympic team."

"Oh, man!" The small man seemed to sense an extended conversation and interrupted before the two men could say anything more.

"Scuse. Many pardons and thank you for your assistance, but we are having to finish and go now."

"Oh, okay. We'll see you later and good luck." The small man managed a strained smile as the stranger walked back toward the other loading dock. Mr. Brown started helping the other four men carry the pole out in two sections. "Hey!" the stranger called to the loading dock bunch as he made his way toward him. "They're getting a basketball goal; it's not fertilizer or prophylactic. They're a basketball team! They're not terrorists!"

After the men had hastily piled into their van and left, the chicken truck had come and gone and the rest of the Loading Dock bunch had dispersed, Purdie Mae stood out on the loading dock smoking a cigarette while Gene broke down some boxes for the dumpster.

"I wonder what she's up to?" Purdie Mae asked as Gene finished the last box and passed by her on his way to the door.

"Who?"

"Oh, that rich old biddie, what's her name? Misenheimer?" She stammered a second as she searched for the name. "Ah, I don't know her name but she's been sitting across the road staring at us since the supposed terrorists were here." Gene walked up beside Purdie Mae and stared down the alley toward a shiny black Lincoln Navigator that sat across Main Street. A woman wearing dinner plate sunglasses sat behind the wheel looking toward them.

"I don't know but maybe she ought to take a picture."

"Yeah," said Purdie Mae and waved exaggeratedly toward the woman who turned back to face the windshield. "Hey!" The woman sat there for a few minutes and then drove off. "I don't know," said Purdie Mae, sending a plume of smoke skyward, "Maybe she's tailing those fellas. Thinks they're terrorists too."

IX
Stake Out

Marilyn was sure they were terrorists! Over the last couple of days she had come to grips with the fact that she wouldn't know a terrorist if it bit her on the butt, but she couldn't shake the fact that the men whom she had seen in the motel parking lot had been Muslim extremists.

The entire night had been a bust. First off, Mitchell had come out of the bathroom smelling like whiskey sour and High Karate so she had him wash up and brush his teeth. Then she found that he hadn't shaved, he wanted that rugged and untamed look, so she had him go back into the bathroom and do that. Then he had trouble getting her bodice off. Then he had trouble unsnapping her garters. After that everything he wanted to do either tickled, hurt, or concerned covering her with an oily slippery substance that three times that evening sent her into the bathroom to wash it off. By the time that she got back for the third time, he had gotten dressed and was busy gathering together all the apparatus that he had brought and was preparing to leave. He went outside and sat in the car while Marilyn changed her clothes; she left the little outfit he had bought her in the bathroom trash can and joined him. There was very little conversation on the way home. Marilyn asked him if he wanted to get some ice cream; he said no. She asked him if he wanted to rent a movie; he said no. After they got home she asked him if he wanted a drink or maybe some coffee. He said no and skulked down to the den where he turned on a ball game. He didn't come to bed until three that morning and, when he did, Marilyn snuggled up beside him hoping that maybe they could make love in a relatively normal way and that might smooth things over. He turned his back to her, however, and went to sleep, leaving her lying there staring at the ceiling and dreading the next visit to Dr. McCandless.

Earlier that evening as Marilyn and their youngest, Martin, watched *Mousehunt* and she halfway listened for the sounds of Mitchell's footsteps on the basement stairs, she kept thinking of the men that she had seen in the motel parking lot. They were definitely Muslim, at least the first man was. When she had first seen him, he was kneeling on the ground pressing his forehead to the pavement. She had seen whole crowds of people do that on television. They had to do that four or was it five times a day? She wasn't sure but that's what he was doing; she was sure of that. Then there was the language that the little man was shouting when he came to get the first man. It sounded so foreign, so angry and the mere sound of it made the hairs on the back of her neck stand on end, even more than Mitchell's plans for the evening. But what were they doing in Ashewood Falls? Welbourne County has never been what you would call cosmopolitan. Over the last couple of years a few Hispanics have trickled into some of the local communities, but not many, not like it's been in other parts of the state. Then there are one or two Orientals, and a doctor from India, but no Arabs. Marilyn couldn't remember ever having seen anybody from the middle-east around here until that night and she couldn't help wondering what they were doing here, and if what they had planned was all together decent.

The next day, Mitchell had left without a word again and Marilyn drove over to the Old Toll Road House. The exterminator that the Historical Society had hired, without her input of course, had said that there was major termite damage to the underpinnings of the house. Marilyn had had dealings with Tony Dorsett before and knew he was about the dumbest person that the Lord God had ever stretched skin over. Now that Slobber McAllister was dead, Tony was eclipsed in stupidity only by his son T.J. and Marilyn wouldn't trust Tony to wash her dog, much less let him have the final word in such an important matter as this. She had driven out to the house to crawl under it and see for herself.

When the Cloud Nine appeared on the side of Adam's Ford Road in front of her Marilyn decided to look around and see if the men were still there or if they had moved on to do their do their evil somewhere else. She pulled in and instinctively came to a stop in front of the room that she and Mitchell had stayed in the night before. The curtains were still drawn, as were the curtains in the room next door that the men had been or were staying in. The van was gone. As she scanned the breezeway and the parking lot to make sure that no one was going to see her there she noticed that someone was leaning against the wall beside the door to the other side of her and Mitchell's room. He looked like the bum that Wade Burgess had chased out from in front of the church the day before for panhandling. In fact, she was sure of it. He was short, small-boned and dirty. He had long stringy hair and a beard. Marilyn thought that he looked a little bit like Charles Manson and he was wearing a long, blue coat with a hood that looked out of place on him. She tried not to make eye contact but they did for a brief second and he smiled and gave a sly little wave like he knew who she was, what she was doing and, even worse, what she had been doing there the previous night. She turned away, threw the Navigator into reverse and floored it when she heard the squalling of tires and looked to her left to see an orange van that had almost t-boned her. She could see that the men in the van glaring out at her through a dirty windshield were Arabs. The passenger side door opened and one started to get out when Marilyn floored the Lincoln again, backed into the parking space behind her and flew out of the parking lot leaving a vapor trail of blue smoke behind her.

She didn't slow down until she had pulled the Navigator down the driveway and around back of the Toll Road House. She watched the road for a good fifteen minutes before she got out of the car. She wasn't about to go under the house like she planned. She could just see those men catching her while she was in that crawl space and slitting her throat; it would be the perfect hiding place for the body, or maybe they would burn the house down around her. They would probably rape or torture her before they did. She had heard stories about what happened to those poor women who lived over there, forced to hide their faces in public, treated like property. These men wouldn't hesitate to kill her, especially if they saw her as being in the way of whatever insidious plot they were hatching. She didn't go under the house, but shined her flashlight underneath at the beams and, as she had expected didn't see anything, typical of Tony Dorsett. She made a note to call Dr. Beck and tell him to find someone else to give them a second opinion and, after getting back into her car, headed home; but she changed her mind before she was even out of the driveway and decided to go find Phoebe Farley. She hadn't seen Phoebe since she had broken the news to her about their husbands and she wanted to know how everything was working out. Besides since her run in with the Arabs, she didn't want to go home alone.

She pulled out onto Adam's Ford Road right behind two teenage girls in an old MG. As they both neared the motel, the van pulled out in front of the MG so that the teenagers had to slam on the brakes to keep from hitting it. Marilyn held her breath as the girls blew their horn and shot the van the finger. In her mind Marilyn could see the back door come open and one of the men machine gun them all. She whispered to them to be quiet and breathed a sigh of relief as the MG pulled off and the van stayed on Adam's Ford Road as it passed the Ashewood Falls city limits sign. The problem now was that she was in full view of the van, although the occupants didn't appear to notice her behind them or didn't recognize the car and she decided to take advantage of their obvious carelessness and follow them to see what it was they were doing in Welbourne County. She followed them downtown and parked on the side of Main Street while the van went down a back alley behind Brown Home and Hardware. As she watched, she could see very little of what the men were doing, but she did get a clear view of Purdie Mae Pearce and some of the crowd that was always hanging around that grease pit she called a restaurant. Tony Dorsett was among them and so was the little vagrant from the motel. *First off,* she thought to herself, *how did he beat us here and, secondly and most importantly, was he involved?* He was a stranger just like they were and she had heard tell of Muslim terrorists using people who appeared American or even disguising one of their own to appear American. *But what about the rest?* As bad as they were, they weren't terrorists. In fact, and Marilyn was loath to mention this, the rednecks of this town were often times more patriotic and more civic-minded than the supposed upper crust, a fact that put a lot of the movers and shakers in this town on the outs where Marilyn was concerned. They were like the mayor and his bunch, which, yes, included Mitchell, who were content to sit back on their laurels, sip pina colada's at the country club, play golf and socialize while probably the biggest diamond in the rough in the state, Welbourne County, sat stagnant letting the world pass it by. Marilyn had known from the first time that she had set foot here that this place was a gem. It had great natural beauty that, in her opinion, rivaled New England, where she had grown up. Welbourne County had the nicest people, among whom she was never included, and, most of all, it was a historic gold mine which nobody seemed to pay any attention to. They were too busy with their social lives. For all these reasons Marilyn was tempted to actually vote for Purdie Mae when she had run for mayor against Farley a couple of years before. She had been tempted to the point that she stood in the voting booth for ten minutes until Mitchell started rapping on the curtain telling her to hurry up. She had voted for Farley in the end. The thought of having such an ill-mannered completely tasteless harpy like Purdie Mae as mayor was just too much to bear.

Marilyn watched the van back down the alley onto Main Street and drive away toward Welbourne Avenue. Even after it had disappeared around a corner, she still stared, wondering what to do. Should she keep after them? She knew where they were going or where they would return to after awhile: The Cloud Nine Motel; but the men could be dangerous and it wasn't her place to try and apprehend international terrorists, and what about the man with the beard and raincoat? How close was he to them, or was he connected and would it be any safer to follow him? Sure, he looked harmless, but so did the blind sheik in the Santa Claus hat and sun glasses who bombed the World Trade Center the first time. The bum might be going back to the Cloud Nine as well, so she could stake out the motel, but again that job wasn't hers and it was one that she definitely wasn't qualified for. She could call the police, but the last thing she wanted was to be labeled a crack pot. She was still deep in thought when she heard somebody yelling: "Yoo-Hoo!" She looked down the alley and saw the ill-mannered, completely tasteless harpy wave at her as if to let her know that she had been discovered. She rolled up the window, slipped her sunglasses up onto her nose and pulled away from the curb, still not sure what to do.

X
THE Jesus

The stranger showed up on Monday just as suddenly as he had the day before when Daniel looked up from his injured finger and saw him panhandling in front of Central Methodist. He was coming back from his usual lunch at The Spider's Delight, a burger joint that catered mostly to Woolman students and staff. He had just turned off Woolman Row onto College Ave. and was about to turn into the College's maintenance complex when there he was sitting on the curb, the hood of his raincoat pulled up over his head and his "Hungry Pleeze Give" sign lying on the sidewalk beside him. His head was bowed and he was watching the water from the morning's rainstorm rush into the storm drain near where he sat. Daniel turned into the parking lot, and looking into his rearview mirror, was somewhat relieved that the man didn't see him, or didn't act like he did. When he got out of his truck, however, Daniel stood there in the parking lot and watched the man. He had his hand down past the curb where Daniel couldn't see it but he seemed to be making a stirring motion with his arm, like he was playing in the water. Curiosity killed the cat and compelled Daniel, who was late back from lunch as it was, to walk over and see what the man was doing.

"Hey, Daniel." the man said and in that moment, for some reason, Daniel remembered that he had never told the stranger his name.

" Hey uh... how you doin'?" Daniel stammered and leaned over the man to watch what he was doing. He appeared to be stirring the dirty brown water with his finger.

"I'm great. Thanks for asking." The man continued to look down and continued stirring.

"I saw you at church yesterday."

"Yeah, I saw you too. You should have stopped and said hello."

"And give you a little cash to tide you over?"

"Oh, no," the man looked up at Daniel and smiled, squinting into the sun which shone over Daniel's shoulder. "I don't need any money. I just do that to test people."

"Test people?"

"Yeah, I'm sort of an expert on human behavior so I just like to do that from time to time. You know, take a sign that says you're cold and hungry and stand out in front of a church where a lot of rich people are supposed to be worshipping the Lord, who I might add preaches generosity. It's very enlightening and it kind of reminds me of that old joke somebody told me one time."

"What joke is that?"

"Sit down and I'll tell it to you." Daniel looked at his watch. He was now fifteen minutes late, but he did make his own hours and, for some reason, he didn't want to go back inside. The day was perfect and the morning rain had given it that fresh smell that the stranger had talked about a couple of days before and, besides, he wanted to hear what his new friend had to say. He looked down at the curb beside where the stranger sat. It was awfully wet and the water still gushed by in the gutter where he would be putting his feet, but he struggled down, trying to put his feet over the water into the street and keep from falling flat on his back in front of God and everybody. "Okay."

The stranger started his story and leaned over against Daniel like he was sharing a secret; Daniel held his breath to keep from smelling him. "This preacher dresses up like the devil and stands beside the driveway to his church and, as people come in for the eleven o'clock service, he tries to tempt them not to go in. 'Don't you want to go home and go back to sleep?' He'd say or 'The race starts early; today don't you want to go back home and skip church?' Well, all the parishioners are having a ball and they're laughing at the preacher and he's having fun tempting them and feels like he's getting his message across when this car pulls to a stop. The driver's side window rolls down and when the preacher goes over, this old guy behind the wheel says, 'I'm glad to finally meet you. I've been married to your daughter for twenty years.'" The stranger elbowed Daniel sharply in the ribs and started laughing in a high pitched, weezy-sounding laughter that lapsed into a snorting fit.

"That's pretty good," Daniel said chuckling to himself. After a few minutes of listening to the man laugh, he pointed to the sign lying face up on the concrete. "So, are you conducting an experiment here as well?"

"Oh, yeah. You know that you've got a lot of young people on this campus who are real quick to stand up for these humanitarian causes: affirmative action, peace in the Middle East, famine and the AIDS crisis in Africa, helping free that Black Panther who shot that cop in Philadelphia. What's his name? Mummy? Mumia? Whatever. They're quick to grab their signs, march, cuss, throw rocks, cause a ruckus, but they won't give a bum a quarter. You stand there with your sign and your hand out and they just drive on by in their BMW or stick a cell phone that Mommy or Daddy bought them in their ear so they don't have to listen to you. You see that won't get them in the paper, or on television. They can't put that on their resume." The mere thought made Daniel smile. It seemed that there were protests on campus every weekend that regularly stopped traffic or damaged property so that maintenance would have to go out and fix it, but in all their self righteous furor, they wouldn't give a vagrant twenty-five cents.

"So, which group is harder to deal with?" Daniel grinned. "These students or Wade Burgess; you know he had words with you yesterday."

"Oh, it's always better to be cussed out than ignored. At least Wade saw a problem and confronted it rather than pretending that it wasn't there."

"Yeah, well, Wade can be a little hard to deal with."

"Wade's a sad person. He's the classic case of someone with so little self-esteem that he uses confrontation to make up for it. He's really a lonely little boy wrapped up in that big body."

"We all thought that when he married Jane, his wife, he'd calm down."

"Well, he has, hasn't he?"

"Yeah, well he did for awhile."

"He's gotten used to having her around now. He's quit putting on airs on her account, but I think that he still loves her. What time is it?"

"It's a little past 2:20."

"Well, I've done enough sitting around; back to my experiments. There's a ministerial association meeting at the community building." Daniel got to his feet and watched the stranger stand as well.

"You sure you don't need any money?" he asked and tried to swallow his words as soon as they had tumbled past his lips. He wasn't sure what he wanted the stranger to say, but, as he refused, it was a relief none the less.

"No, I'm okay."

"Good," Daniel said and started to walk away.

"But I do need a place to stay."

"Hmm." Daniel turned and started walking toward the building, knowing what he wanted to do but knowing that he shouldn't. He looked back, hoping that the man would be gone, but he was there, sign in one hand and using the other to pat his pants and coat pockets like he was looking for something. Daniel called to him, hopeful that he wouldn't be heard, but the man turned and, shading his eyes with his hand, looked his way. "You don't have a place to stay?" Already his inner voice, which for some reason always sounded like Wade Burgess, told him to walk away, to go inside, get to work, and not to associate with the man again.

"Well, I was living at this motel right outside of Ashewood Falls, what's its name? The Cloud Nine? It doesn't look like the place for me, real shady you know."

"Yeah, I'll bet."

"I moved out this morning. I figure that I'll find some new digs sooner or later." As the thought, the reckless, irresponsible, stupid thought began forming his head, that voice, that Wade Burgess sounding voice, began screaming at him like Wade had done on so many occasions. *Don't do it! Don't do it! Don't do it!* The voice between his ears grew more and more distinct as the thought tiptoed down behind his forehead, his eyes and his nose to his throat where it got a running start and flew, not with the total blessing of their master right out of Daniel's mouth and into the stranger's ears.

"I guess you could move in with me for awhile." *Noooooooo.* The voice faded away in a fury like the Wicked Witch of the West melting into her trapdoor in *The Wizard of Oz,* but Daniel's apprehensions were still there and he argued with himself about whether to recant his invitation when it was scarcely out of his mouth or to insist that the stranger become his new roomie. Mostly he just prayed that the stranger would give him the easy route and say no, which he didn't.

"Yeah, okay, that'd be great. It won't be any trouble, will it?"

"No, no trouble at all; just as long as you work my little act of kindness into your experiments. Make me a variable on the side of the good people."

"Oh, you already are," the stranger said, tugging on the lapels of his coat. Daniel smiled in spite of himself. The look on the stranger's face was so warm, so friendly and so earnest that it was hard not to.

"One thing, I do think that I should know your name if we're going to be sharing a house."

"Oh, of course. My name's Jesus." Daniel was almost floored by not only the stranger's statement, but also by the fact that he had just agreed to have a lunatic stay at his house. He stood staring at the man who stared back with the same friendly expression on his face. Daniel knew that he had to say something and he stammered for awhile, fishing for the right phrase.

"Is that Hispanic? Like Hey-Soos or something?"

"No, it's Jesus."

"So you were named after THE Jesus huh?"

"I am THE Jesus." If the stranger's previous statement had floored Daniel, this one wiped the place with him and for the rest of the day until the stranger stepped into Daniel's house that evening, he regretted even speaking to the man initially. He didn't want this man in his house, but he also knew that he couldn't turn the man away. That wasn't a viable option.

"Well," Daniel stammered. "I guess we won't be short of wine, will we? We've got a whole lake of water, or are you just going to walk across it?"

"You know I'm not much of a show off." The two men had steadily moved closer together as they had been talking, and now the stranger got shoulder to shoulder with Daniel again. "But I was messing around a little before you got here. Check out the water in the drain if you're thirsty."

Because of an unfortunate lay of the land, there was pretty much always water pouring into this particular storm drain, especially for a few days after a rain and the shower that day had ended not an hour before. The landscaping needed to correct this problem was number one on Daniel's list of problems for maintenance to correct, but it was forever put off by easier jobs which always pushed the landscaping down to number two, if only for a day or two, only to have it pop back up into its initial designation. The fact that the stranger would suggest that Daniel drink that water curled his lip up and turned his stomach. The water was nasty and a repository for all sorts of flotsam including, but not limited to paper, food, pieces of decomposing animal, beer bottle caps and used condoms, picked up by this miniature Mississippi along its route as well as dumped into it by students. The color normally ran the gamut from army cot green to baby doo yellow, but as Daniel studied it that day it looked different somehow. He knelt down to get a closer view and could see that it was clean. Not only did it have a golden color, it sparkled in the sunlight and tiny bubbles rode the crest of the torrent before disappearing into the drain. If he hadn't known better he could swear that it was wine instead of water.

"I've got some running around to do." Daniel was distracted by the marvel that was running through the gutter in front of him and the stranger had to repeat himself.

"Yeah, okay," Daniel said, still staring down.

"You get off at five right?"

"Yeah."

"Can I just meet you here?"

"Sure."

"Bye." As the stranger wandered off down the sidewalk Daniel knelt down closer to the water and then moved back to the other side to let the sun shine on it and see if it was a trick of the light, but it still had that golden sparkly look to it. Daniel looked up and down the street and, seeing no one other than the stranger who was just about to disappear over a slight rise, he put his hand down into the water and held a handful up closer to his face, letting it pour out between his fingers. It looked the same, so he got another handful and held it up to his nose. It had a slight smell, but it wasn't the usual stench that the water brought with it; he thought that it smelled a little like wine. He stopped for a moment and let that handful run out. He put his hand back into the water and let it run over it for awhile before he scooped up some more and brought it to his lips.

"What the hell are you doing?" Daniel dropped the water and looked up to see Wade Burgess looking down at him from the driver's side window of his truck. Daniel thought quick, which wasn't a talent of his, and dreamed up a story. He was pretty proud of himself after that.

"Just checking the water; looks like somebody might have dumped something into it."

"You were gonna drink it, weren't you?"

"No, just smelling," Daniel said, standing and shaking his hands to dry them off. "Sometimes the students dump stuff into the storm drains, bubble bath, dye, anything to be cute. It can get into the water supply, so we have to watch it."

"See anything?" Wade asked.

"No, looks clear. Probably some food coloring or a shirt or something where the dye bled off." As they watched the water, which was now a deep tan in color with dark flecks of trash, a tampon floated by and balanced on the storm grate for a second or two before disappearing beneath it. "What brings you by?"

"We're practicing tonight at seven at the lanes."

"Sounds good."

"I'm going to get them to set up the pins on one lane in a 6-10 split so you can just shoot at it. I don't want you costing us a win next season." Daniel rolled his eyes and turned away as Wade gunned the engine and sped off. He dreaded it already. He'd be shooting at the same baby split all night while Wade bellowed at him each time it wasn't perfect and the more he drank the louder he would get. That was another thing that Daniel dreaded. Since he had drunk the water out of those beer cans, he hadn't touched alcohol: no beer, no wine, nothing, and he hadn't wanted to, except for whatever was in the storm drain. In fact, the mere thought of swilling booze turned his stomach.

When he got back to his office he looked at the clock on his computer; less than five hours to go before he'd have to deal with Wade. He remembered when he liked to bowl; he remembered when he liked hanging out with the fellows at the lanes which was the only reason he had started bowling in the first place, but now it was all nothing but a drudgery. Bowling was like boot camp and any socialization would involve alcohol, which would, in turn, lead to some of Wade's mess. He didn't want to go but he had to and he was getting tired of things, of situations that he had to do or had had to take part in. He pulled his cell phone out of his pocket and dialed Lisa's number. He got James Earl Jones again, telling him that the Verizon customer he was trying to reach was not available at this time. He hung up and flung the phone across his desk where it came to rest against the last picture that he and Lisa had had made together. He wanted to call her and tell her all his problems, about Wade, about how nothing is really as enjoyable as it once was, and he wanted to tell her that he had quit drinking. Sure she'd say "again?" but she'd also tell him that she was proud of him and that she loved him or at least she used to say things like that. Now he was lucky if he got a "hello" out of her. He also thought that he ought to tell her about his new house guest, but in the mood he was in, it didn't matter. Would she mind if this vagrant stayed in their house for a few days? Hell yes, she'd mind, and for that the idea of Jesus coming to stay with him suddenly became very attractive. Yeah, she would hate the fact that Jesus was staying in their house just like she'd hate the fact that Daniel gave him his raincoat, but, seeing as she wasn't around, Daniel guessed that the decision was his and his alone.

XI
6-10

Jesus stood in the kitchen and watched Daniel leave for the bowling alley just like Daniel had watched Lisa drive away a couple of days before. When he and Daniel had returned to the McDaniel house there was a message on the answering machine from Lisa. She said that they had finished up early in Raleigh, but that something had come up in Pinehurst which demanded their immediate attention and she would be a day or two longer returning home than she had initially planned. Daniel called again and again got James Earl Jones, so he threw the phone onto the counter and plugged it in to charge up the battery.

"It's kind of tough being away from family, isn't it." Jesus said as he looked around the den.

"Yeah. You're not married, are you?"

"No, and it gets old real quick being alone, don't you think?"

"I guess not. Why don't you have any disciples anymore?" Daniel was mostly kidding, his statement being just something to say rather than a serious question.

"Oh, well, they don't make men like that anymore."

"What do you mean?"

"Do you want to be my disciple, Daniel? Would you follow me unconditionally? Could you follow my advice or my word without question?"

"Okay, I follow you." Daniel had to look toward the floor as he walked into the den to join Jesus. When he finally looked up, the man's face was neither angry nor judgmental, but he was smiling with that same fetching grin.

"That's okay. There aren't that many, and even if I did get some people together, we'd probably either be boycotted by the ACLU or raided by the government so it's better to work alone these days." Daniel nodded and smiled, but as he showed Jesus the spare bedroom, the bathroom where the fresh towels were located, and the soap, emphasizing soap, he couldn't help feeling embarrassed for himself and ashamed for the world that he had lived in so comfortably for so long. While Jesus was getting settled in, Daniel changed clothes for his three hours of hell at the bowling alley and then they sat down to frozen dinners and small talk until it was time for Daniel to go. As he was putting his bowling bag into the bed of the truck, he looked to the kitchen window to see Jesus watching him go. They exchanged smiles and waves, but the whole thing made Daniel uncomfortable, partially because it was a man watching him go instead of his wife and then again because she wasn't there to do it. As he pulled out onto Old Mocksville Highway, he tried to call Lisa again and got her voice mail again, which put a big chip on his shoulder before he even got to the bowling alley and an even bigger "kiss my ass" on the tip of his tongue as Wade met him at the door to tell him that he was five minutes late and that his first 6-10 was already set up.

"You need to get moving," Wade said as Daniel worked on a knot in the laces of one of his bowling shoes.

"Well, you know," Daniel shot back as he freed the knot and slipped his foot into the shoe, "I don't think those pins are going anywhere. Do you?"

"Well, what's wrong with you? You must not be getting any."

"I think Lisa's out of town!" The mayor chimed in.

"Well, maybe the lack of sex will make him bowl better," snapped Wade as Daniel stepped onto the approach, set his AMF Beast onto the ball return and began to dry his right hand over the blower. Daniel picked up the first 6-10.

"Okay again!" Wade ordered and Daniel bit his lip as he and Mitchell Misenheimer gave each other the "our friend is a jack ass" look that they all gave each other when Wade was up to his usual crap.

Daniel spent the next hour shooting at 6-10's with Wade yelling "Again!" after each from the next lane where he and the other two actually bowled and seemed to be having a much better time. One time the "again" was conspicuously absent, and, when Daniel looked in Wade's direction, he found all three of his teammates looking toward the front desk where The Four Horsemen were signing up for a couple of lanes. Whereas Birddog Realty was the perennial champs of the league, the, Horsemen were the turkeys. Captained by Purdie Mae Pearce, who was allowed to bowl on a men's league only after several near violent fits and a threat of legal action, the Horsemen also included Rufus, Tony Dorsett, not the football player the exterminator, and his son T.J.

"Okay, boys, the pros are here!" Wade bellowed, obviously making sure that the Horsemen heard him. "Let's watch. We'll learn something!" Daniel turned away to throw at his next split. He was just as quick to laugh at some of Wade's antics, especially when he was getting onto Purdie Mae Pearce, but a lot of times, like now, it was just embarrassing. As he picked up the next 6-10 Wade shot back one more comment, "Yeah, same to you! Ugly old cow!" Daniel made three more splits and Wade told him that he could go get a beer.

"Oh, thank you, Great One," Daniel muttered as he passed by Wade who appeared not to notice. Daniel stood on the walkway beside the table where Mitchell and the Mayor had been smoking.

The all-to-familiar pitcher of Bud and four paper cups sat on it like a handful of religious knick knacks spread over an altar. The mere thought of drinking even a drop of beer still turned his stomach and, as he stood there, he looked down into the pitcher through the golden, foamy liquid and first realized how close it did resemble urine, in color and smell. At that moment he wouldn't have been surprised if it had tasted like it as well.

"Hey, Danny Boy!" Daniel looked up to see Wade glaring at him from the approach, purple Rhino in hand, "it's for drinkin', not for looking. Now chug-a-lug. You need to loosen up!" Daniel shot him a look that could have killed lesser men but again it bounced off Wade like bullets to Superman. Daniel picked up the only cup that hadn't been drunk out of, filled it, and brought it to his lips as Wade turned around, but he didn't drink. "Okay now hit some more of those pins."

As Daniel plodded down toward the approach he looked over his shoulder and noticed, for the first time, that the Mayor was in some sort of heated discussion with Tony Dorsett. The rest of the Horsemen stood aside and listened in, but it was Tony who seemed to be doing the talking. As Daniel got up to shoot at another split, it was time for the Mayor to bowl and Wade began hollering for him after his customary two second wait had elapsed. "Birddog! Hey, Birddog! Where are ya!" As Daniel began his approach, he could hear Wade bullying his way onto the conversation which he did with all the couth and tact of a bull in mating season. "Hey, you idiots need to leave the mayor alone and let him bowl! Whatever business you have can wait! You'll get your welfare check or whatever else you're wanting!"

Daniel turned around and shanked the split, much like he had done the last night of the season and he quickly hit the sweeper button so Wade wouldn't see the miss, even if Wade was chest-to-chest with Tony Dorsett who came up about to Wade's arm pit. Daniel turned around and faced the lanes as he waited for his ball to return, mostly so he wouldn't have to see the confrontation. He didn't feel like seeing Wade bully yet another pipsqueak. Just as he got ready to release the ball, Wade's voice rattled the windows like thunder, "Terrorists!" Daniel shanked another split. "Boy you people are stupider than I thought!" Daniel forgot bowling for a few minutes and walked to the beer table so he could hear what was said in the conversation at the back. As he got there Purdie Mae waded into the fray with a stiletto like fingernail all ready to thrust into Wade's face. Daniel had to smile at the anticipation of it all.

"You listen here," Purdie Mae shrieked. "He knows what he saw and we're just trying to do our duty as citizens. If we see anything peculiar, we're supposed to report it to law enforcement or local government. I heard Tom Ridge say that himself on the T.V. just the other day."

"He was telling people that who live in New York, Washington D.C., Chicago, big, important cities. Not Ashewood Falls, North Carolina! Good grief, you morons can't get your panties in a bunch just because a bunch of Mexicans ride through town in a van!"

"They weren't Mexicans!" Tony yelled, struggling to match the volume of both Wade and Purdie Mae. At this point it appeared that the argument was turning into just another one of Wade's conquests, so Daniel went back, hit the sweeper button and prepared to shoot at the next split. "They was Afganeranians! I talked to 'em myself, and they were asking a bunch of questions!" The mayor tried to get involved in the conversation then and was prepared to ask Tony the same question that Wade did, although he planned on using a great deal more professionalism.

"Just what sort of questions do terrorists ask? 'How do you get smallpox out from under your fingernails?' How about 'Watch my camel, will you, while I run in here and plant a bomb or two?"

"They was asking about the Cloud Nine Motel and then I saw two of 'em downtown and they was asking about the federal building."

"Oh, no!" Wade screamed and jumped back in mock terror. "They're gonna blow up the Cloud Nine and the Farm Bureau! How will we ever cope? Oh, it'll be anarchy, anarchy!" Mitchell started laughing into his beer and the mayor, still trying to play the professional, cupped his hand over his mouth.

"Wade Burgess, why do you always have to be such a complete jerk!" Purdie Mae shot back at him. "What right do...."

"Because I get tired of dealing with incompetence, especially when it comes from a bunch of ignorant white trash and an ugly old bat like you!" Daniel was just about to release his bowling ball; he had hit three in a row during the fracas when a loud pop rang out and he put the ball into the gutter. He turned around to see Wade, his face as red as a monkey's butt, rubbing one cheek.

In their attempt to break up the ensuing melee the mayor was kicked in his sore knee, an old war injury and one of Mitchell's eyes were blacked. The hoo doo went on for at least five minutes and only stopped when the Mayor screamed, "Cease and Desist!" All in the building stopped including those who didn't know what "cease" or "desist" meant, which, as it turns out, amounted to most everyone in the building and looked toward the little group, which until then had escaped their notice. "Wade!" the mayor screamed. "Go Bowl! And you!" He turned to Tony and took a few seconds to calm himself down and regain his professional demeanor. "Next time you see something suspicious, call the sheriff. They're the ones who are qualified to handle something like this. Thank you for your concern."

Daniel had moved back up onto the approach as the crowd dispersed and, as Wade stepped up onto the opposite approach, the mayor limped to the beer table. Daniel turned around and shot at the next split. He hit the six on the left side but it bounced around the ten, missing it totally.

"Oh, come on! "Wade groaned." Haven't you learned to hit it yet?"

"I'd say I have. I've hit most of the ones that I've shot at."

"Well, you need to hit some more." Daniel had planned on doing just that, but since Wade had ordered him to do so, he said, "No" and stepped down off the approach, ball in hand. "I'm tired of splits. I think I'll shoot some strike balls."

"You're gonna get over here and shoot at splits until you can do it right!"

"No." Daniel strolled around to the other side with his ball under his arm. As he passed near them, he heard both Mitchell and the mayor groan.

"Come on, Dan," the mayor moaned. "We've had enough of this

for one night."

"And I've had enough of his crap for a lot longer than that." Daniel said, stepping up onto the approach and coming within inches of Wade. He had never felt this good before; he had never felt this bold where Wade was concerned. He liked it.

"Boy, you're not worth a damn! You know that?" Wade said backing up an inch. "Can't bowl, you're too much of a wussy to drink a beer with us. No wonder your wife is bumping uglies with another man!"

"What did you say?" Daniel asked as his face grew hot and began to get as red as Wade's one cheek already had.

"Come on, Wade. Just let him bowl," Mitchell said as Wade dismissed him with a wave of his hand.

"I said that it's no wonder that your wife, Lisa, you remember her, is fooling around with another man. If you had just a little bit of a backbone about you..."

"Take it back."

"What," Wade got that obnoxious, amused grin on his face and looked behind Daniel at the mayor and Mitchell like he always did when he was starting something. "I'm not taking back anything. Now get back....." Wade glanced again over at Mitchell and the mayor, who had come down into the well for some show of solidarity. He got very little if any. At that moment Daniel raised his ball over his shoulder and spiked it into Wade's foot like a football. Wade shrieked like a schoolgirl and raised that foot just as Daniel connected with a kick worthy of Mia Hamm into Wade's groin. Wade's shriek ended with a choke and a gurgle. He dropped to his knees with both hands firmly planted on his twig and berries and cracked his chin on the ball return. Daniel stood looking down at him, his anger abating as quickly as it had come when he heard the sound of someone clapping. He looked a few lanes down where the Four Horsemen had been practicing and saw Purdie Mae standing on the approach, beaming and putting her hands together. Within seconds the clapping grew and pretty soon the entire building was roaring with applause except for Daniel, Mitchell, the mayor and Wade who was laying on the floor in a fetal position, crying.

The house was quiet when Daniel got home, no TV, no radio, which he was pretty well used to as much as Lisa had been away, and Jesus sat on the couch drinking a glass of water. He was looking toward the door when Daniel entered like he had heard him drive up. He smiled that same cordial grin as Daniel slid his bowling bag up next to the bar, walked into the den and flopped down in his Lazy Boy.

"Hard night?" Jesus asked.

"Yep," Daniel leaned the chair back and thought about going to the refrigerator for a beer, out of reflex mostly, and then decided not to.

"Trouble with Wade I'll bet."

"How'd you know?" Jesus simply shrugged his shoulders and smiled.

"Oh, yeah," Daniel nodded and then stared at his feet propped up on the foot rest for a few minutes before he spoke again. "I hurt him."

"How so?"

"I dropped my ball on his foot, on purpose, and then I kicked him in the nuggets."

"Ouch, that's not good."

"Now that I've calmed down I feel bad about it all. I shouldn't have lost my temper."

"I think that losing your temper is excusable; the violence is where you made your mistake."

"Well, I shouldn't have blown my stack in the first place."

"Everyone loses his cool." Jesus sat his glass down on the coffee table and turned in his seat to face Daniel, who was feeling better just from the attention. "It's human. No one has an infinite amount of patience."

"Except maybe Job, right?" Daniel chuckled, proud of himself for his ability to draw on a biblical example.

"Yes, Job was very patient and he was loyal to the Lord even after he lost everything, even when he had absolutely nothing material to gain, but he did waver. He did question God's will to the point that God had to remind him who was boss."

"You never lost your temper."

"I didn't?"

"You did?"

"Yes, I did. Remember the money lenders in the temple?" Jesus registered the blank look on Daniel's face and then reached for the Bible on the coffee table. It was the big white one that he and Lisa had gotten for a wedding present. He couldn't remember the last time that he had looked at it. Jesus opened it to the page he wanted first try and then handed the book to Daniel. "See here," he said, pointing to Mark 11:15 with a very dirty fingernail. The verses told the story of Jesus chasing the money lenders out of the temple, of turning their tables over and stopping anyone from bringing in any more merchandise to sell.

"Wow, hardcore," Daniel said as he scanned the book again.

"See, I lost my temper; and if I can, then I should excuse that in everyone. I will not fault you for becoming angry. I know Wade asked for it. Where you were wrong was turning to violence. A fact that I think you know and the fact that you are remorseful says something in itself, although you should be thinking about making amends." This statement made Daniel feel even lower because he had the opportunity earlier in the evening as he was driving home. Mitchell had called him on his cell phone and had given him the same old excuse that they always gave every time one of Wade's tirades was directed at Daniel.

"He's just being Wade. You know that," Mitchell had told him, the tone in his voice sounding like it was all Daniel's fault that Wade was being a jerk.

"Wade can go straight to Hell!" Daniel had told him. "And if that's what you think, you can go with him." Remembering this made Daniel feel even worse and he stared at the floor, unable to look directly at Jesus. He prayed that he wouldn't find out, although he was pretty sure that he already knew.

"You shouldn't feel bad about standing up to Wade. In fact, you should be applauded especially after his treatment of some of the people in the bowling alley. It took courage for what you did. I know how you feel about Wade and I know that you don't like confronting people, but the essence of being a Christian lies in the courage that you exhibit and the whole act of becoming a Christian and worshipping God takes courage and large amounts of it. In today's society it is taking more and more courage to be a Christian as more and more people seek to inhibit a Christian's right to worship the living Christ. In the beginning, being a Christian was punishable by death. For a Christian to openly accept God when he knew that he could be fed to lions took incredible courage and, again, I don't want to brag, but it took courage for me to spread my father's message when many people, many powerful people, wanted me dead and it was made worse by the fact that I knew from the beginning that they would succeed. Daniel, as you become closer to God, he will test you. He will test your courage among other things and it won't always be easy. There will be many times when you are expected to dig deep and to show this courage that I am speaking of.

Remember, we want you to stick up for yourself and your beliefs; we just can't condone the violence Tonight's little problem can easily be put behind you and I think that you know how." They both sat in silence for several minutes and then Jesus got up, drained his glass, stretched and yawned. "Well, I know this is all a lot to digest, so I'll let you sleep on it. I've got a busy day tomorrow so I think I'll call it a night."

"More experiments?"

"Oh, yes, a big one. The biggest since I've come to town." Daniel didn't answer but stared though the glass door at the lake and the blinking red light on top of the radio tower reflected on the water. "Oh and Daniel."

"Yeah?"

"I'm proud of you." The statement was so corny. One grown man telling another grown man, who wasn't even related to him that he was proud of him. What made it even more corny was the fact that Daniel was glad he had said it.

XII
I Am Tater!

"That Wade Burgess!" snapped Purdie Mae as she slammed a piece of chicken down into one of the fryers, splashing grease as far as the counter and burning all, the Dorsetts, Stanley, Gene, Rufus and the stranger, who sat there. "If there is anybody in this world that I would love to shoot between the eyes, it's him."

"So does this all mean that you finally believe me?" asked Tony rubbing his wrist.

"No, I can't say as I do. I think that it's awfully far-fetched that we have terrorists in Welbourne County. If they attack, like the old jackass said, they're gonna attack a big city where they can kill a lot of people at once. What you gonna blow up in Welbourne County that can kill a hundred people, much less a couple thousand, 'sides the K-Mart?"

"Listen, I know what I saw."

"I know you know what you saw and I don't wanna hear another word about it. If I hear one more word about terrorists or Wade Burgess, I swear to God I'm gonna fillet somebody." As Purdie Mae slid a knife through a breast of chicken to emphasize the point, the door opened and the cowbell that hung over the door clanged as it had done everyday for the last twenty years. Purdie Mae looked past the crowd at the counter towards her new arrivals, and the look on her face warned the rest that everything was not all as it should be. "Hep ya?"

"Yes, please." The man's thick Arabian accent told all at the counter who he was, especially Tony. T.J. just sat staring into the mostly empty basket in front of him. The pattern of ketchup, salt, bits of French fry and wrinkles on the wax paper looked a lot like the asteroids game on the old Atari that his dad had set up in the den at home. "We are wanting some food."

"Well, uh, have a seat and we'll be right with you." The whole crowd watched the five Eastern men like hawks, as they had done the day before at the loading dock. As the newcomers approached a table, the short man stopped beside the chair at the head as if he were waiting for something. Another one, the youngest, pulled out the man's chair, put an ornate box onto it, grasped the man under the arms, sat him on the box, and pushed the chair back under the table. As the small man straightened himself on his box, Purdie Mae got five menus out from under the counter and brought them to the table.

"What can I get ya'll to drink?"

"We will all take water," the short man said. The others sat quietly. Three, including the short man, had their hands clasped together. The other two, as Purdie Mae could see when she laid down the menus in front of them, each had one hand on the table and were holding hands underneath. She figured that the shrimp must have seen them as well because, as she was walking back behind the counter, the man slapped the table with the palm of his hand and the other men brought both hands up like the rest. After he had let them sit for a few seconds, the small man nodded and they all opened their menus at the same time and began looking them over. The fact that all the people at the counter had been staring at them was not lost on the men, although they pretended not to notice.

"I'm surprised they're drinking water," Stanley whispered to Gene as Purdie Mae sat down their glasses. "I thought that it'd be Pepsi; you know, Osama Bin Laden owns stock in a company that produces some kind of gum that they use in making Pepsi Cola. Makes a killing off....."

"Shhh!" Purdie Mae cut him a look as she walked to the men's table, order pad in hand. "What can I get for you?" she said, stopping beside the little man's chair and taking a pencil from her bouffant.

"Tell me," the man said snapping his fingers. "Is there anything that you serve that is pork?"

"The only thing that we have that's pork are the pork chops. Have a taste for pork today, do we?"

"Oh no, no, no," the man said as if Purdie Mae just asked if he could fly. "Our religion prohibits the consumption of pig meat."

"Oh, well, that's the only thing that you have to worry about. Nothing else has pork in it."

"Are you sure?"

"Yeah, I'm sure."

"Do not lie to me woman! I need to know this! The meat of a pig cannot touch our lips!"

"I'm not lying to you! I should know what's on my menu! You

know I'm fixing to cram..."

"Here, look at this! This word here! What does it say? Ham?"

"That's a hamburger! That's not pork, it's beef!"

"Beef?"

"Yeah, you know. Cow meat."

"Then why does it say ham?"

"Damn if I know, but it's not pork!" She went over to the counter and took the basket with Gene's half-eaten hamburger in it and brought it back to the table. "See here, this is a hamburger. Does that look like pork to you?" The man examined it, pushing his face down close to it like he was studying the Koran.

"What are these?"

"Those are buns. The hamburger comes between them. They're bread, no pork."

"And these?"

"Those are French fries, they're potatoes, and this red stuff is ketchup which is made out of tomatoes."

"And this what is this? This is pink like pork!"

"That's the gum that Gene was chewing. He put it there until he was done eating."

"You are sure this is not pork!"

"Yes!"

"Then we will all have the hamburger."

"Y'all want cheese on that?"

"Yes, yes."

"And what else?"

"I am not concerned with that woman," the man said, sending Purdie Mae away with a condescending wave of his hand. "Do not bother us. Now away." Purdie Mae snapped up the menus, making sure to accidentally pop one of the men in the forehead as she relieved him of it. As she stomped past the counter, slinging the menus onto it, all there including the men at the table could hear her muttering.

"... kick his ass so bad his mama's gonna feel it." When she disappeared through the swinging metal doors, the dining room was quiet except for a periodic slam or curse coming through the serving window. All those at the counter had spun around on their stools to stare at the men at the table, who still seemed oblivious, until the short man slowly turned his head and met all their glances with his own.

"So quiet in here. When we came in there was such a bustle of activity and talk. Now you just sit there like your tongues have been cut out. We walked in on a private conversation?"

"Oh, no, we were just talking about terrorists," the stranger piped up like he was talking baseball with someone or other.

"Ah, terrorism. The subject that is on the lips and minds of all Americans these days. With all the horror that the rest of the world has suffered, you Americans suffer one tragedy and already you are experts, martyrs to a way of life that you seek to push on everyone else."

"And if some of the people living over in your part of the world," Tony began sliding off his stool like he was ready for a showdown, "learned about our way of life they may start demanding it!"

"Demanding what? The freedom to sin as they please? To turn their back on their creator?"

"God gave us free will for a reason," The stranger stated, drawing surprised looks from all in the room. The short man turned in his chair to respond but Tony cut him off.

"How can you compare a roof over your head, Papa John's whenever you want it, and the freedom to say and do whatever the hell you want, to fried lizard, a mud hut and the threat of getting your tongue cut out and your wife raped if you....."

"We live the way Allah wishes us to live and we will be rewarded in the afterlife. Why don't you infidels stay away from our part of the world and keep your sin from corrupting us."

"Our sin! You're the ones coming over here flying our planes into skyscrapers, trying to poison the water and food supply! It makes me laugh to be called a sinner by a damn terrorist!"

"Oh, now it comes out! Some Middle-Eastern men come though your town, and right away you enlightened Americans start assuming that we are terrorists! This is what they speak of! What do you call it? The ethnic profiling! We are being harassed because of where we come from!"

"If it looks like a terrorist and sounds like a terrorist and smells like a terrorist, then chances are it's a terrorist!" By now Tony was up against the short man's chair and the shrimp had climbed up onto his box so he could look eye-to-eye with Tony. The rest of the men just sat and stared except for the young man sitting beside the short one, who stood up like he wanted a fight. This brought Rufus off his stool and he walked up behind Tony and announced that he had his back. All the rest stayed where they were at the counter. T.J. continued to look into his basket.

"Can I ask you something?" asked Purdie Mae as she approached the table with the men's hamburgers. The short man waved her away as if Purdie Mae's decision to speak would be in anyway hindered by the fact that he didn't want her to. "What are ya'll doing in town? Do you have business here? Or are you just passing through? We just don't see too many Arabs around here."

"Like the man at the store told you yesterday, we are a basketball team. We are the Olympic team representing the Republic of Yemen."

"And do you play?"

"Yes, I do."

"Honey, we all know that's a bunch of bunk. "Purdie Mae looked over at him with one hand on her hip. "You're barely tall enough to tie your shoes."

"I am the point guard!" he said, raising his fist as if he had just claimed Welbourne County for the nation of Islam. "I am the swing man! The speed demon! The perimeter shooter!"

"And why are you in town? You putting on an exhibition or something?"

"We are playing the Devil Deacons."

"The who?" Tony scoffed and looked back at the rest of the crowd, who started snickering.

"The Devil Deacons. The team from the University, Wake Forest."

"You mean the Demon Deacons!" Tony corrected.

"That is what I said. We sent letters to all the major colleges in the country and all but the Devil Deacons have refused. They are terrified at the very thought of facing us. In fact the Devil Deacon's men are so frightened to face the Yemish team, they are hiding behind the women and sending them to play us."

"You mean to tell me you are playing the Wake Forest Women's basketball team?"

"That is correct."

"You gonna get murdered," said Rufus, who still stood behind Tony.

"We will be victorious! This will just be the beginning. We will take what we have learned about the American basketball programs back with us and we will form a program that will crush the American team. The, as you say, Dream Team will be demoralized as will be your entire infidel nation!"

"Let's beat the hell out of them and throw them out of here!"

shouted Rufus and, reaching over Tony's shoulder, took hold of the short man's t-shirt, a purple one with the Powerpuff Girls on the front of it.

"No," Tony said and pushed Rufus' hand away. The short man fell back, but the younger man caught him and prevented him from falling off his perch. "Hold on a second. If you're a basketball team, prove it."

"We do not have anything to prove to you! Trash!"

"No, I think you do. I don't think you're a basketball team. I don't think that you'd know a basketball if it bounced up and bit you! I think that this bunch here could beat y'all at basketball."

"We would bury you!"

"Like I said, prove it! Bring it on!" The man looked into Tony's eyes, which stared back, unblinking, burning with determination, anger and the small touch of insanity that said he might be capable of anything. The man glanced back at his men; three sat just as they had been since they came into the place, the other stood behind him staring at Tony in much the same way as he glared at the short man."

"Okay, we will do it!"

"Good, meet us at the Mann Commons at 3:00 this afternoon. You know where that's at?"

"We will find it. Bring your best infidel!"

"You're going down, Akbar!"

"I am not Akbar! I AM TATER! And that is a name that you will not soon forget."

"He's right," squeaked Gene. "It'll be a long time before I do."

"We must go and prepare. We will be at this Mann Commons at three."

"Meet us at the court, Muhammed." The short man slid off his box and motioned for the young man to pick it up and for all of them to follow him toward the door.

"Hey!" Purdie Mae called after them. "How about these hamburgers?"

"We will not be eating them."

"Well, you still have to pay!"

"We'll pay if your team wins today."Purdie Mae growled as they left and, as they were crawling into their van, she went into the stockroom and emerged with the sawed off .12 gauge that she kept back there for just such emergencies.

"Where are the shells?" she demanded, checking the chamber.

"There are a couple in the cash register," Rufus called over his shoulder as he went to the window and watched them drive away. "But I wouldn't worry about it now, they're gone." Purdie Mae hissed through her teeth and slid the gun onto the counter.

"Say, why'd you let them leave?" Rufus asked Tony as the later joined him at the window. "Between all of us we could have taken 'em."

"I know, but the problem is bigger than us. We can't just beat the tar out of them and then throw them out. That doesn't stop what else they've got cooking. If they're out to cause some trouble or kill a mess of people, kicking them out of here won't stop them from setting off a bomb somewhere or putting something in the water, taking some hostages, whatever. We've got to get something on them, some evidence so when we go to the police, like the mayor said, we can prove what they're up to."

"And we can do that by playing them in basketball?" Gene asked.

"Yeah, well, the basketball game's a distraction. All we need then is somebody to check their van or maybe their motel room while they're playing us."

"We need more than that," said Gene. "We need some players."

"We got some. There's you, me, Stanley that makes three. Hey, how about you?" He pointed to the stranger who appeared to have been deep in thought and jumped at the act of actually being spoken to.

"Who? Me? Well I guess I can. I'm not doing anything this afternoon. Sure."

"Cool. Then there's Rufus, that makes five. That's all we need. It's all they got."

"Now I don't know about all this," said Rufus, shaking his head and leaning a long lanky arm on the counter. "This don't sound like something that I want to get in the middle of."

"Oh, come on, please," begged Tony. "We need you; you'll be an important part of the team."

"Well, I can't play basketball."

"Sure you can you're tall."

"It takes more than being tall. Shawn Bradley's tall.

"Yeah, but you're black."

"And Manute Bol was tall and black." Rufus was starting to get an edge on his voice, which was normally as smooth as silk. "Now don't start stereotypin' me now."

"Come on, Rufus, please. We need your help in this. Like I said, the whole plan could revolve around you. Think of your country."

Early that afternoon Tater ordered his men to keep practicing and went inside for a drink of water and to pray. For the last couple of hours something that men his size carried around in their stomachs, and men like Tater suppressed, had been growing and growing until it was getting a little hard to ignore. That was doubt, and, as he watched the men through the window practice passing in front of the basketball goal that they had bought the day before, he couldn't help wondering, for the first time since he was a child, if they would succeed. He wasn't worried about the basketball game; they would win, there was no doubt about that. What worried him was another infinitely more important cause.

XIII
Back To Nature

Since her latest inspection of the Toll Road House was far from what she had intended, Marilyn Misenheimer went back. This time, however, she went back armed. Mitchell had lots of guns, mostly shotguns and rifles that he took hunting, and then he had a .38 that he kept in the glove compartment of his truck. The gun that Marilyn brought, the one that she was least afraid of and that she could get out of the house without Mitchell finding out, was one that he had won at the previous year's Harvest Festival.

The Sons of Confederate Veterans had a booth on the sidewalk in front of the courthouse and were raffling off a pistol, which had been custom made to coincide with the release of *Outlaw Josie Wales* on DVD. It was a gun similar to the one that Clint Eastwood carried in the movie where each chamber had to be loaded by hand with a small paper packet filled with gunpowder and a ball-shaped bullet. Then a lever was pulled down to pack the wads into the chambers. For some reason, unknown to her, Mitchell had insisted that Marilyn learn how to shoot, not only the 30.30 that he kept in their bedroom closet, but the .38 and the Josie Wales gun, as she called it.

Nobody was home when Marilyn left, so there was no problem in getting the spare key to the gun cabinet from the desk in Mitchell's study and slipping the gun into the oversized purse that she carried on occasion. She did have to meet Mitchell at the park that afternoon, an appointment that she dreaded like a pap smear, but she was pretty sure that she could get the gun back where it was supposed to be without him knowing it was ever gone.

As she passed the Cloud Nine, she tried to take a glance in the parking lot and not slow down. The glance she got was fleeting, but she did get a look at the van and the Arabs who were out in the parking lot, and it looked like they had put up a basketball goal and were playing basketball! She pushed the pedal down a little farther and sped up so that she almost missed the Toll Road House driveway and squalled tires as she whipped it in and pulled around to the rear. She ran to the corner of the house and stared at the road for a good fifteen minutes to make sure that she hadn't been followed. She cursed herself as she stood there, cursed herself for burning rubber and making so much noise. *They could have heard that,* she told herself, and they could come and find her here alone. Sliding a hand into her pocket book until it came to rest against the hilt of the gun embossed with Clint Eastwood's face gave Marilyn some sort of comfort. They couldn't see her back there, and if they did try and come, she could probably pick a couple off before they even got out of the van; if she were under the house, shoot! That would be better. They'd only have one way to come in and she could pop the first face that looked in at her.

She watched for a few more minutes and then hurried to the crawl space door. It was still standing open from the last time that she had been there, and the area underneath the house looked pitch black, almost as if she jumped in, she would fall forever. She didn't want to go in, but she had to make herself. This was for history; this was for all those residents of Welbourne County who had fought and died and worked their fingers to the bone; this was for the Hessian and his ladylove and Mitchell's great-great-great uncle who had died at Antietam, whom Mitchell had never given a rat's patootie about; this was putting off getting to the park to meet Mitchell for at least a good half hour. She was close to being late then, but he would just have to wait and, as she fished around in her pocketbook for her flashlight, she was still debating as to whether or not she would go at all.

Marilyn got down onto her hands and knees and crawled into the darkened space underneath the house, the gun in one hand and the flashlight in the other. The crawlspace wasn't as dark as she expected, as beams of light coming in through holes in the mortar of the foundation and down through the floor illuminated large sections of the dirt floor underneath. The darting beam of light from her flashlight did a lot to give her a quick assessment of the space beneath the house. It did little, however, toward giving any detail, such as the identity of the small black shape that scurried off to her right making shuffling noises in the damp earth. Marilyn sat back on her rump and turned both her flashlight and her gun in that direction, but whatever it was had already disappeared behind one of the brick supports bracing the floor of the house. She sat there for awhile and then very slowly, very deliberately, began inching forward with the hand holding the flashlight pressed firmly under her nose against the strong smell of mildew and rot that seemed so powerful that she could almost feel it like a slight breeze against her face. She rested on her knees and switched hands so that she could shine her light along the wooden beams above her head. She examined them, even taking time to poke and prod them with the barrel of her gun and hated to admit it, but Tony Dorsett was right. The beams were eaten up with rot, and as she poked one with the pistol, a fine sawdust and larger pieces of wood fell down in front of her eyes. She tried to push the barrel in farther and pry a larger piece of wood loose so that she might be able to get a look deeper into the wood and see if there was also a termite infestation. As she was leaning forward on her knees and pressing her face close to the beam, a granddaddy-long legs crawled up underneath her leather mini-skirt and crept across her bare bottom. Marilyn let out an ear splitting screech that the Arabs did hear back at the motel, but ignored. Marilyn fell back onto her backside, squashing the spider, the gun discharged blowing the beam that she had just been looking at to bits and allowing the body of a badly decomposed cat to drop down and hang by its tail mere inches in front of her eyes. The gun fired again, reducing the cat to small bits of bone, hair and dried flesh that sprayed all over her like confetti. The scream that followed did not quite match the first in volume, but should not be underestimated. All in one motion Marilyn flipped over onto her all fours and galloped out through the crawlspace door like a racehorse, stopping to scream again as a large possum crawled across her right hand on his way out in front of her. She didn't stop until she was sitting against the front left tire of the Lincoln. She was able to get to her feet, but shot out her side-view mirror when her cell phone rang. She stood there with a white-knuckled grip on the flashlight and a still smoking pistol as the phone rang on and on until she was able to collect herself, reach into the car and answer it.

"Where are you?" Mitchell snapped. Marilyn was able to settle down and gather herself as her husband called her name four more times over the pop and crackle of the cell phone. She looked down over her skin-tight halter that was smeared with red mud. She looked at her skirt with a rip up the side clear to her waist. She looked at her fishnet stockings, similar to the ones she had worn at the Cloud Nine, and saw runs up the front of both. She had taken off the stiletto heels when she went under the house but had stepped on both and broke the heels. She could only imagine what her face and hair looked like.

"Mitchell," she said, already dreading his reaction. "I don't want to do this. Not today."

"Whatever," he said with a sigh. "It's up to you." And then there was a short silence before he asked if she would just see him at home. The silence was the worst of it. Because, although he didn't speak a word in those few endless seconds, he said an awful lot that only his wife could have understood. In that silence he told her that he was very disappointed, that what he had asked of her shouldn't be that big of a deal. What was a little potential embarrassment to make the man she loved feel a little more wanted? Feel like he was the center of her universe, just like it was just after they had gotten married. It was something that she could do for him. It was one thing that they could share, that would be between the two of them. Basically, and Mitchell never said this nor did the marriage counselor, it was all Marilyn's theory, but she believed that Mitchell needed a little proof of how his wife felt about him. No, she did not believe that they had grown apart, not emotionally; they had just grown used to each other. Dr. McCandless had told them jokingly that women marry men hoping that they will change and that men marry women hoping that they will never change and that everybody ends up disappointed. Yes, Mitchell needed to see his wife make an effort to please him again, like she hadn't in almost ten years, even if it was something that she didn't necessarily want to do.

"I'll be there in a few minutes," she said, trying to sound cheerful and get the shiver out of her voice. "No, that's okay. I'll see you in a little bit. Okay, I love you, too: Bye." Marilyn tried her best to clean herself up with a box of wet ones that she had in the car. She brushed her hair, put on fresh make up and was able to brush some of the dirt off her clothes. She just took off the hose and left the heels where they lay at the crawl space door; she would have to go with the barefoot look. Then she crawled behind the wheel, checked her face one more time in the mirror and headed to the Mann Commons. She was thinking of her husband as she passed the Cloud Nine and didn't notice that the Arabs were gone and so was their van.

IX
Air Jesus

The Mann Commons is a twelve acre park on the outskirts of Ashewood Falls' downtown district. It's bordered by Depot Street and the new Welbourne County Courthouse to the north, Welbourne Ave. and the old courthouse to the south, by the new Hatcher county complex and Phaegan Road to the east and by a Western Auto to the west. The surge in governmental growth that produced the aforementioned buildings, except for the old courthouse and the Western Auto, of course, began a good five years before the first ground breaking when then clerk-of-court Billy Sykes came into her office early one morning and found about an inch of guano on her desk blotter. Being an energetic, ambitious and pushy woman, she brought the matter before then county manager and her father-in-law, Saul Sykes, who ordered an investigation as to the condition of not only the courthouse but the county office complex which sat directly in front of it. The results of the investigation were distressing to say the least. The courthouse was not only infested with a huge colony of bats, but inspectors reportedly found rats the size of Chihuahuas in a rarely used basement, silver fish were as thick as fleas on a hound's back in vital records, and a bum named Rooster had been living in an out-of-order men's room just down from the board of education for, according to Rooster, at least two years. There was a severe mildew problem in both buildings, which contributed to a high instance of respiratory problems in long term employees, of which there were few. There was asbestos in the courthouse, and the county building sagged at one end to the point that everything in the parole office that could roll, including but not limited to pencils, pens, office and wheel chairs, would end up in one corner.

The decision to build another courthouse and county complex was not a hard one and, spurred on by Mrs. Sykes and her father-in-law, went to a vote just a little over a year later. It passed by a landslide, but it was four more years before construction started because there were very important issues to be considered first. The builder was a hurdle that was easily jumped. White's Builders and Construction, Inc. was the only builder in the county and a trusted name in the area. The architect was a harder decision, since J.W. Mann, former mayor of Ashewood Falls who still had a seat on the board of county commissioners and was a force to be reckoned with, pushed hard for the board to hire his nephew Bernard who had graduated from an unpronounceable little college in Mississippi with a degree in architecture the year before. The rest of the board was inclined to go with Wendy Byrd. Miss. Byrd was not a resident of Welbourne County, coming from Charlotte, J.W.'s main arguing point, but, unlike Bernard, graduated from N.C. State, a university that everyone had heard of and, unlike Bernard, had proven to be a very competent architect, having designed the main branch of the Charlotte City Library, the Children's Museum in Raleigh and another museum in High Point dedicated to the history of the textile industry in the Piedmont, N.C. The debate was long, drawn out and heated, and eventually led to the resignation of J.W. Mann from the board of commissioners and the hiring of Wendy Byrd to design both the courthouse and the county complex.

When finished, the new courthouse, a five-story glass and steel structure, actually sat with its back to Depot Street and faced the old county courthouse, a classic old columned building of yellow brick which sat across Welbourne Avenue. The old courthouse was gutted, cleaned, and the necessary repairs were made to it. Then it was padlocked and sat empty until it was acquired by the historical society. Plans to open a new museum dedicated to the history of the county are presently underway. The new county office complex was built across Phaegan Road instead of in its previous location, so the old building was demolished to make way for a city park, an action placed before the board of commissioners as a way to appease J.W. Mann and honor his sister, Ophelia who was another one of the county's elite. She had died the previous January. The completed park stretched between the two government buildings. Welbourne Ave was rerouted so as to go behind the old courthouse and not disrupt the sloping green lawn giving the entire scene a look reminiscent of the Mall in Washington D.C. that lies between the Washington Memorial and the capitol building.

Other than the scenic beauty that the park brings to Ashewood Falls, it also boasts playground facilities, a snack bar, a gazebo and a bandstand which allowed for speakers and music. On a perfect spring day, as the high school band played *On The Wings of a Snow White Dove,* a tearful J.W. Mann thanked all the citizens present for making Welbourne County the little patch of heaven that had meant so much to his sister and meant so much to him as well. He offered the Mann Commons as another little patch of heaven, their present to the citizens of the county who could come there and socialize, be entertained and bask in God's glory.

"You know, my sister didn't smile much when she was alive," he said, wiping a tear with his handkerchief and drawing a good deal of laughter and nods of agreement from the crowd, "but I can't help thinking that as long as a park is here with her name on it for people to come and enjoy themselves, that she will be smiling an awful lot." That statement drew polite laughter and applause, although all who were there, Mr. Mann included, knew that if Ophelia Mann were to look down, or up as the case may be, and see a lot of people relaxing and playing in her park, then she would probably be more apt to say something to the effect that they should all get jobs than to even think of smiling.

Included in the playground facilities are a Little League baseball park and a black-topped basketball court, both with bleachers for spectators. Tater and the rest of the Yemanese Olympic team parked their van in the parking lot above the basketball court and filed down a concrete runway onto the blacktop to stare at the Welbourne County Boys, as Tony had dubbed them, across the cracked white line that designated center court. They were wearing dark green uniforms that looked to be made out of silk or a similar fabric and the numbers on the jerseys, the trim on the jerseys and shorts as well as the Arabic writing across their chests were done in gold. Their basketball shoes were also green and had the crescent shaped symbol of Islam on each side.

The Welbourne County team was far less equipped. Tony was wearing his trademark Tony Dorsett, the football player, #33 Dallas Cowboy's jersey, warm-up pants and twenty year old Air Jordans. Their star center, Rufus, was wearing his dark blue pants and work shirt with a Misenheimer Industries iron on patch over the breast pocket, wrap around sunglasses, an Atlanta Braves baseball cap and steel-toed work boots. Stanley Fisher was wearing what he had put on that morning: black bat-man t-shirt and camouflaged pants. He had changed out of his combat boots and into a pair of red Chuck Taylors. Gene was wearing a "Quilter's keep you in stitches" T-shirt, safety goggles, checkerboard Van sneakers, and a pair of warm-up pants whose string had been lost years before. The result was a good four inches of vertical smile anytime Gene did anything but stand up straight. The stranger, the man that Daniel McDaniel knew as Jesus, was wearing the same thing that he had been wearing since he had arrived in town except for the rain coat; he had left it with Purdie Mae who was sitting in her and Rufus' car in the parking lot just a few yards to the other side of the Yemanese team's van.

"So, here we are," said Tater, addressing Tony as the rest of the team from Yemen stood behind him in a straight line, feet apart and hands clasped behind their backs.

"We were beginning to think that you weren't going to show up."

"So you hoped."

"Yeah, sure," Tony said sarcastically. "Let's do this."

"You have ball?" Tony looked embarrassed for a moment and then looked back at his teammates, who returned similar expressions.

"Is all right," chuckled Tater. He snapped his fingers and Bubba stepped forward with a basketball that he had been cradling under one arm.

"So, who shoots first?" Tony asked.

"Jump ball?"

"Who throws it up?"

"Muh, I mean, Skeeter, will; he is good at this." Tater gestured to the man over his right shoulder.

"How do we know he'll be straight? My boy T.J. is over there." Tony pointed to where T.J. was sitting on a bench staring blankly into a laptop. "He isn't even playing."

"How do we know he will play it straight?"

"Oh, for God sakes, Tony," Rufus groaned. "Just let the visitors take the ball first like in baseball." Tater grinned and nodded what seemed like miles up to Rufus, who towered behind Tony.

"All right. It won't help them."

"How will we keep score?"

"T.J.'s doing it by computer." Once again Tony gestured to his son, who hadn't moved.

"You will forgive us if we keep our own count," said Tater and, as he snapped his fingers, Skillet held up an abacus.

"Suits me." Without another word both teams went to the other side of the court, except for Rufus who stayed beneath the goal where Tony told him to stay.

June Bug in-bounded the ball to Skillet, who sent it back quickly. Then June Bug flipped it past a dozing Stanley Fisher to Bubba, who rocketed it down the court to Tater, who had snuck past the defense and was streaking down the court as fast as his diminutive legs would carry him, which, as it turned out, wasn't very fast and the ball passed by him so he had to run faster to catch up with it. He grabbed it at the top of the key and put the ball up just a few feet in front of the basket, where Rufus sent it back at him with a volleyball-style spike. The ball hit Tater square in the face, setting him on his butt, and bounced back up into Rufus's hand. Rufus, not knowing what to do with the ball, sent it toward the other goal baseball-style missing it by a good foot, but Jesus was able to catch it in mid-air and lay it into the basket.

Tater was slow to get to his feet and he saw the word "Wilson" in front of his face for a good week. He made a few steps toward the other end of the court only to be run over by Gene and stepped on by Bubba, dribbling hard toward Rufus and the basket. Rufus came out to meet Bubba, hand raised in an attempt to block the shot, and tripped over Tater. This freed the lane and the basket for a tomahawk slam and two points from Bubba. At this point both teams ran down to the other end of the court, including Tater, who had gotten to his feet and limped along just behind Gene, who had yet to get all the way to either basket. Rufus had stayed under the basket where Tony had told him to stand. The ball was left bouncing just behind Rufus where it had come down after Bubba's slam dunk. The first person to notice his team's mistake was Jesus, who grabbed Tony by his shirt as he passed by him and directed him down to that end of the court where he in- bounded it to Jesus. Jesus vaulted over Tater, weaved between Skeeter and June Bug and began a fast break down to the other end of the court. Bubba picked him up just the other side of mid court and stayed with him until Jesus checked up a good foot beyond the three point line and sank the jumper. The next time down at the other end, Bubba was able to get an alley-oop from Skeeter for another two. At the other end Jesus was able to get a Tony Dorsett pass, which bounced off Gene's stomach and hit another jumper from the top of the key. As the Yeman team attempted to in-bound the ball, Jesus was able to intercept Tater's pass to Bubba for a quick lay up and another two. On the next trip down June Bug went for a lay-up only to be hacked on top of the head by Rufus' fore arm and laid out flat of his back. The ball was grabbed by Stanley Fisher, who was able to get a rather clumsy pass to Jesus, who executed a textbook finger roll for two more points. As Stanley and Jesus jogged down to the other end of the court, June Bug still lay on the ground crying and Skillet cradled him in his arms, making cooing noises and kissing him on the forehead.

"Is foul!" Tater screamed poking Tony in the stomach with his finger.

Hey, shrimp," Tony said pointing back down to him. "These are American rules; no blood, no foul." Standing apart from the action, Stanley leaned forward on his knees and wheezed through his mouth. When he was able to talk, he reached up and put a hand on Jesus' shoulder. Jesus' skin shone with sweat and his hair appeared somewhat damp but he was no where nearly as bad off as Stanley or Gene, who had taken the opportunity to rest and was laying down across one free throw line on his back gasping for air like a fish out of water.

"Man, you are good," Stanley said and then had to double over and gasp for a few more minutes before he could continue. While he panted for breath, Jesus patted him gently on the back. "How'd you get so good?"

"Clean living, my friend," Jesus said modestly. "And a good pair of sandals don't hurt."

"You must be in zone today, or something."

"I try and live in the zone. Everybody should."

X
Rendezvous At The Park

Sex in public is the third most popular sexual fantasy among men: that is, according to a *Maxim Magazine* article that Mitchell had showed Marilyn a couple of weeks before that fateful day at the park. Marilyn didn't know what the top two were, and she didn't want to know. She pulled to a stop in the parking lot at the Mann Commons, checked her hair and makeup in the mirror, and looked down at her clothes which still had smears of red dirt, dust and cobwebs. She slid her sunglasses up farther onto her nose, looked around the parking lot and got out of her Navigator quickly, still glancing around her to make sure that no one she knew saw her parading around the park looking like a street walker from Cornfield County. She padded quickly around the dirty orange van beside her, stepping gingerly as small gravels dug into the balls of her feet, and ran right into Purdie Mae Pearce who was standing behind the van with her hand on the handle like she was about to climb inside. Marilyn couldn't do anything except stare, because, at the moment that she saw Purdie Mae and registered who she was, she realized who the van belonged to. She hadn't noticed it before because she had been worried so much about Mitchell's little scheme, but she knew it now as she made the connection with the nasty color of orange, the patterns of rust, and the little heart shaped window. The van belonged to the terrorists, and here was Purdie Mae about to get into it!

"What are you looking at?" Purdie Mae growled, stepping back, jerking her hand off the van like she was trying to act casual.

"Sorry," was all that Marilyn could say and tiptoed past her toward the edge of the parking lot. Marilyn had had battles with Purdie Mae before and normally would not have hesitated to trade barbs with her; in fact, she was one of the few people in town who wasn't afraid to do so. The fact that the terrorists were there, however, and that Purdie Mae was that close to their van dissuaded her. Plus she wanted to get whatever Mitchell wanted to do over with, with as little pain, mental and physical, as possible.

Marilyn reached the edge of the parking lot and stopped to rub her feet. She heard some loud shouting, and, recognizing one of the voices, she looked down to see the Muslims on the basketball court. They were playing basketball and they were playing against, of all people, Tony Dorsett, Purdie Mae Pearce's lapdog Rufus, and the rest of the bunch who hung around the Poultry Palace! *What in the world is going on?* She asked herself as she watched them. The terrorists were wearing actual uniforms, and while she was watching, the derelict whom she had seen around town lately hit a jump shot. She could say a lot about Purdie Mae's crowd, but associating with terrorists? They were weird, but not that weird, were they? Would they actually associate with a group that wanted to kill Americans? Purdie Mae Pearce had run for mayor a couple of years before and had lost, but that didn't mean that she had aspirations of overthrowing the government, did it? Was she bitter? Well, she was always bitter, but was she bitter enough to associate with Muslim extremists to advance her own agenda? And what about the rest? Did they feel that way or were they going along because Purdie Mae asked them to, or made them? And what about the stranger?

"Hey!" A familiar voice pulled her from her thoughts. "Marilyn!" She began to look around and finally saw Mitchell walking toward her on a little rock path that led off to her right. He motioned for her to come with him and as she reached him and tried to tell him what she had seen, he grabbed her by the hand and pulled her along after him. They followed the path behind an old out-of-service caboose that reportedly had come from the same train as the dining car that served as the front dining room of the Dog and Shake. Initially the caboose had been kept open, but it had become a favorite make-out spot for local teenagers, so it had been padlocked and now served as no more than an attractive backdrop to the basketball court and the jungle gym that sat between them.

Mitchell led his wife up a slight incline into a grove of maple trees to a square-shaped hedge that concealed a rarely used bench. They entered the hedge through a small wrought iron gate and Mitchell pulled Marilyn down onto a quilt that he had spread on the grass beside the bench. On the bench was a bottle of wine and the picnic basket from home. Marilyn leaned back as her husband kicked off his shoes and settled in beside her. Although the hedge concealed everything from them she could still hear the sounds of the basketball game.

"Are you sure you want to do this?" she said, somewhat perturbed that Mitchell had not commented on the condition of her clothes and the location of her shoes and hose.

"Yeah, I'm sure," he said, nuzzling her neck.

"We might get caught."

"Well that's the whole thrill of it all; the danger of getting caught. It adds to the excitement."

"We may have more excitement than we can handle."

"I hope so he said," and lay back onto the blanket, pulling his wife down with him.

XI
The Streak

A half hour later both teams still plodded up and down the court, although the piss and vinegar that they had taken to the court with earlier had been noticeably diminished and the ranks of both teams had been lessened by two. The first to go down was Gene, who ran behind the bench where T.J. sat, still staring blankly into his laptop, fell onto his belly and began puking. Even after the vomiting had stopped, he could only lie on the bleachers, pray and whine about dying and that he was "never gonna get to see Mama again."

The next two went down, one from each side, in one fell swoop. Tony was chasing after Skeeter, who had stolen the ball and was attempting a fast break layup. Rufus had stepped aside to tie his shoe so the basket was left unguarded and the Yemen team would have had an easy two points. It was then that two cheerleaders from Ashewood Falls High School walked by just beyond the goal on their way to the baseball field to pick up one of their little brothers from Little League practice. Their thick, shiny, blond and auburn hair hung most of the way down their backs and their long, smooth looking tan legs moved lithely beneath their short skirts which would flip up every so often and offer a brief but satisfying glance of the shiny red panties that were worn underneath them. It was one such glance that Skeeter was taking advantage of just as he was supposed to go up for his shot. Instead, he just kept on running and centered the metal pole that supported the goal. Tony, who had been taking such a glance as well centered the back of Skeeter. Both were carried off and laid on the bleachers beside Gene, where they held Cloud Nine Motel towels on their bleeding noses and prayed, while secretly enjoying the view they had gotten before the lights went out. Tater himself was the last to go down, poked in the eyes, Moe Howard style, by a woman after he had stepped on her little boy who had run onto the court after his puppy. He was laid on the bleachers next to Gene, Skeeter and Tony, where he held a wet towel on his face, prayed and cursed the day that he had ever come to America.

On the last play of the game, just after Jesus had hit another jumper from the left corner of the court, June Bug in-bounded the shot to Bubba, who was able to get past Stanley and make for the other basket, Jesus sticking with him step for step. He was watching Jesus, as the biggest threat on the other team, and, as he went up for a dunk, took the heel of Rufus' hand right across the bridge of his nose. He was knocked flat onto his back, like June Bug had been, but stood up quickly and stepped toward Rufus until they were bumping chests.

"I am tired of this! You have been doing this all game!" He screamed right in Rufus's face to the point that Rufus' sunglasses started fogging up. "It is foul! It is foul as dictated by the rules of basketball as created by Dr. James Naismith."

"We're playing by our rules!" Rufus shot back, leaning forward so that the two men touched noses. "No blood, no foul!"

"I am hating this rule. I am tired of hearing about it. I will spill your blood so that there will be a foul in this barbaric contest!"

"Go for it!" Bubba's dark, shining eyes widened for a moment and he stepped back a step like he was planning on doing something; a shrill, quivering voice stopped him.

"You will step down!" screamed Tater from where he stood beside the bleachers, the towel firmly clamped on one eye. "There will be no violence today. This is the time for playing basketball! The jihad will not happen now; it will happen in the future and the time for spilling blood will be then, not now! You walk away and in-bound the pass! For the tall infidel's foul we will get the ball back. Surely we are owed that much!" Tater looked to Tony, who was sitting up on the bleachers, towel on his nose, and Tony nodded to him in agreement. "There! It is decided. You will in-bound the pass to Skillet!" Bubba stared at Rufus for a few seconds longer and then walked to where the ball lay on the court and, draping his long fingers over the top of it, palmed it up from the ground. Then he took a step toward the sidelines as if he were going to in-bound the ball as ordered, but instead one-armed it like a baseball, flinging it over the bleachers so that it disappeared behind the caboose.

"You are a disgrace!" shrieked Tater. "Now you will get the ball! You will bring it back and the other team will in-bound it! If you do not stop this disgraceful behavior, you will be off the team! You will be out of the faction and you will be deported to I... I mean Yemen! Now go get the ball! Now!"

Bubba ran past the bleachers and vanished around the corner of the caboose. Tater dropped the towel and walked to where Tony,

Gene and Skeeter sat on the bleachers. "He will be back with the ball soon. We will check the computer and see how bad you are being beaten."

"You can check, Habib," Tony said, removing his towel to reveal a red and swollen nose which was identical to Skeeter's as he removed his towel. They all followed Tater to the bench where T.J. sat and looked over his shoulder to the screen on the laptop. There was no score; only the Windows XP desktop.

"Boy, didn't you start the scoring program?" asked Tony. Despite his disappointment, Tater chuckled at the incompetence of it and gestured to T.J. behind his back.

"Your son is about as smart as a camel dropping," he said. "Let us check our abacus." They all walked to it and, as Tater picked it up, only one bead had been slid over for the Welbourne County team and none for Yeman. "Who was supposed to be keeping score?" Tater screamed, his face turning darker by the minute. The team members that remained just looked at each other and shrugged their shoulders. "Idiots, morons!!!" Tater started jumping up and down like spit a on wood stove. "Now we will have to start all over!"

"Looks like T.J. isn't the only one who's as smart as a camel dropping," chuckled Tony behind the towel that he had put back onto his nose. Before anybody could say anything more, a dog-killing shriek came from behind the caboose and everyone turned just in time to see a woman fly by the bleachers and down toward the baseball field like the devil was after her. She was screaming like a banshee and was completely naked from the waist down. Everybody watched her go as she disappeared into a crowd of Little Leaguers, coaches and parents milling about behind one of the dugouts. In a minute a man came loping along, buttoning his shirt. Just after him was Bubba, who hugged the caboose like he was dodging a sniper and ran to the group with an expression like he had just stared death in the face.

"Allah, forgive us! We have sinned!" shrieked Tater and dropped to his knees, the rest of the Yemen team dropped along with him. "We have gazed on the lustful, naked body of an infidel woman. Oh, Allah, forgive us! We must go and pray and beg for forgiveness!"

"What about the game?" Tony grinned.

"You can have the stupid game! We will forfeit! Our eternal souls are more important than your game!" Then they ran up the hill and disappeared across the parking lot. In a few seconds an engine could be heard cranking up and then the squeal of tires faded into the distance. The Welbourne County boys began hooting, high-fiving and pumping their fists.

"Yeah, baby!" yelled Stanley as he rubbed Gene's belly roughly, causing him to get queasy and sit back down on the bleachers.

"Now, I only hope Purdie Mae found something in that van," Tony said as he walked over and tapped T.J. on the shoulder, telling him to log off of the laptop. T.J.'s fantasy, that he had been living the entire time, where he had led the Charlotte, not New Orleans, Hornets against the world champion Lakers in the hive, faded away just like the Dallas Cowboy's star on the computer's desktop.

"Whether she did or not," said Rufus, "I think she owes us some beers." Everybody cheered and hooted some more at the declaration as they filed up the hill toward the parking lot. As they made their way up the ramp, Stanley looked back for Jesus to ask if he was coming along. He was gone.

XII
Me And Dubya

Sheriff Leo Dorsey kept a picture on his desk, along with photographs of his wife, children, grandchildren and dog, of the President of the United States, George W. Bush. He had gotten it when he, along with several other sheriffs in the area, assisted with security when the President paid a visit to Greensboro the previous year. It was the same picture that you would get of George W., stern look on his face, hawk-like eyes gazing off into the distance, if you were to write to the White House and request a photo, except this one was autographed: "To Sheriff Dorsey, Keep up the good work. Thank you for helping keep our country safe. President George W. Bush."

The sheriff always liked George W. Well he had liked every Republican President since Nixon and he had voted for him anyway, but, here lately, he identified with President Bush, and he had taken to keeping the picture on his desk as inspiration.

The president had been under fire lately for various things; 9-11, the war on terror, Afghanistan and the like, and the Sheriff had taken his lumps as well. Since that high school student got ripped, got naked, and decided to jump up on the computer trailer at the high school, it seemed that the favorite prey for people in Welbourne County wasn't squirrel, rabbit, or even deer anymore. It was the sheriff, the man that a year before everyone had so loved and respected, the man whom the voters had decided would be their sheriff for twenty years in a row, and twelve of those he had run unopposed. They now criticized; they called him "Iron Britches" because of his ever expanding girth as well as his style which was formerly called hard nosed, but now it was arrogant and self-centered. Voters even hinted that in the upcoming election they might decide to retire Ol' Iron Britches and replace him with the Yankee Keith Miller, who Dorsey had actually liked until he had announced that he would be running against him. Keith was a good deputy, but it was getting harder and harder to be business like when he would catch him talking with the other deputies in the halls, or in the break room, telling them that, when he was sheriff, he would do this and he would do that, and, when Dorsey reminded him that the election had not even started, he would reply with, "Just talking Sheriff" or "Got to be prepared, you know, like the good Boy Scout." If he wasn't careful, the Boy Scout would be busted down to being Resource Officer at the High School. Then since he was going to "get tough on this drug problem" he could watch the little bastards and solve the crime from that angle, find out where they were getting their drugs, if he was as smart as he said he was.

Sheriff Dorsey saw this whole drug thing as his own war on terror, and lately his constituents had given him more terror than he could stand. The Meth bust in the old house out on Adams Ford Road had been Dorsey's Afghanistan, a victory and a small assurance that maybe the problem was close to being solved. Then there was the Sheriff's own Bin Ladin, the supply of crystal meth that was still somehow being produced and distributed somewhere in the area. A second meth Lab that had somehow complemented and supported the other one was still functioning somewhere around, if not in Welbourne County. The Sheriff's department just couldn't seem to find the lab, or the people who ran it, or even get hold of a large enough amount of the product to be able to trace back to its place of origin. The longer they went without some sort of news concerning the drug problem, the more intense the pressure got from the people of the county.

One afternoon the Sheriff hung up the phone and picked up George W.'s picture, held it in his lap and stared at it as if it would talk to him and offer him advice. It had been Kevin Miller calling from the Mann Commons downtown. He told Dorsey that Marilyn Misenheimer had been picked up for indecent exposure.

"That can't be who you've got," the Sheriff said and was about to hang up, but the boy scout just wouldn't let it go.

"I tell you that's who we've got," the deputy insisted. "In fact we've got a lot of people down here who are identifying her." He gave the sheriff a description of her: Dark shoulder length hair, sharp features, bitchy expression, tall and kind of hippy.

"That sure sounds like her, but I can't believe that's Marilyn Misenheimer."

"You want us to bring her in?"

"Yeah, you better go ahead." The sheriff groaned as he fished though his desk drawer for a B.C. powder and the pint bottle of Johnny Walker that he kept there. All he needed was another scandal but as he poured the powder into his mouth and reached for the whiskey Miller had some more bad news.

"Say, her husband's down here. You want me to bring him in, too?"

"Mitchell Misenheimer?" Dorsey gasped as he choked down the powder.

"Yeah, that's him."

"He naked too?"

"No, but it seems that he and the Mrs. were doing the wild thing in the bushes over behind that old caboose. He admitted to that. That would be public fornication, wouldn't it?"

"Oh God."

"What'd you say, Chief?"

"Bring 'em both in."

"Gotcha."

When the phone rang again, Sheriff Dorsey was resting the picture on his large belly and staring hard at the inside of his eyelids. He set the photo on the desk very gently, very carefully, as if he were afraid it might break or bleed if he dropped it. He picked up the phone and gave his usual curt two word greeting.

"Sheriff's office." At first there was no response except for a loud rustling noise as if someone had dropped the phone and was trying desperately but unsuccessfully to pick it up again. "Sheriff's office." Dorsey said a little louder and more distinctly this time. Sometimes he got calls from little old ladies about stray dogs or kids bothering them or something and they couldn't hear very well so he had to speak up. He was getting ready to speak again when somebody finally said something on the other end.

"Hello." This didn't sound like a little old lady.

"Yes, sheriff's office. Who is this?"

"Umm, yeah, I-umm-need to talk to the sheriff."

"This is he."

"Oh umm, yeah. How you doin'?"

"Fine, sir, can I help you with anything?"

"Uh, yeah. You know that meth-lab?"

Assuming that this was the infamous meth lab that had been plaguing him for the last month, the sheriff said "yes."

"Well, uh, I know where it is." The sheriff waited on baited breath for several seconds expecting an answer.

"Well?"

"You wanna know where it is?"

"Yes, please."

"There's a duplex over on Fitzgerald Avenue, just behind the little grocery store. You know where that is?"

"Yeah, I sure do," the sheriff said, jotting down the directions even though he had been to the neighborhood more times than he could count for various types of crimes and infractions that needed the attention of the sheriff's department. The neighborhood around Fitzgerald and Commanche Drive, just on the outskirts of Ashewood Falls, was the worst neighborhood in the county, ripe with prostitution, drugs and the occasional murder; and most of the county was content with that as long as the bad element stayed in that neighborhood. It was when it started creeping out into the rest of the county and the population got a glimpse of what the people who lived around Fitzgerald and Commanche saw everyday that everything hit the fan.

"Well, the people that live in both sides of the duplex, you know, they're both in on it."

"Okay, and how do you know this?" the Sheriff asked, but the voice was gone, replaced with a dial tone.

The sheriff didn't even hang the phone up before dialing the squad room and getting a hold of Darnell Hughes, who, due to less-than-ideal grooming habits, always served as a decoy anytime the sheriff's department did a sting operation. He sent Darrell home to put on his civvies and to meet them at the sheriff's department satellite office on Comanche just down the road from the store and duplex that the man on the phone had spoken of. Then he called for back up, which included the Boy Scout. He wouldn't have included him, but he wanted him to see it when it all went down.

"Don't you think that we should stake the place out first?" The Boy Scout asked.

"No," answered his superior. "We don't know who the informant is. He could get caught or have a change of heart and tip us off. I want to act on this thing, so, if you want to be involved in all this, get the Misenheimers taken care of, get them processed and in the lockup, and meet us at the Comanche Road office. We'll wire Darnell and send him in about 6:30. It should just be getting dark, so there ought to be some activity."

"You're the boss," the Boy Scout said. After he had hung up, the sheriff struggled out of his chair, put on his hat and gun belt and gave George W. one more glance.

"Yeah, boy, I am. I sure am!"

XIII
A Real Bad Day

The day that Jesus and the Welbourne County boys were having fun playing basketball and the sheriff was having fun planning his raid, Daniel McDaniel could safely say his day sucked. First off, some students had dropped grow-beasts into the fountain in front of the Administration Building. Grow-beasts are small animals made out of sponge that grow about ten times their size when dropped into water. At least once a year some student would drop a pack or two into the fountain, and sometimes, like the day in question, they would get stuck in the intake, clog up the drain, and necessitate a long and a tedious process to extract some giraffe or brontosaurus. They would commonly get stuck deep in the drain and, in the attempt to get them out, they always seemed to tear so they would have to be removed a bit at the time and it would usually take hours. Of course, as head of maintenance, Daniel wouldn't have to do any of the actual work, but, in problems such as this, where one member of the administration or the other would get their nose out of joint, he would have to supervise.

The process of extracting the grow-beasts had hardly begun when Daniel was called to the gym where Joe Petrella, the basketball coach, launched into a tirade about the walls of the gym, which maintenance had painted the day before, being red on black instead of black on red. Then just as Daniel had returned to his office, he had gotten a call from the Mayor telling him that Wade was just being Wade so just let everything slide and meet them at the bowling alley that night so they could smooth things over. Daniel tried hard to think of something that he could say, something sharp and witty where he could tell them all-Wade, the mayor, Mitchell, all of them-to stick it where the sun don't shine. All he could do was hang up.

Daniel really wanted to talk to Lisa, but he knew that if he got James Earl Jones again that he would spike his cell phone like a football; but, regardless, he sat looking out his window at the maintenance workers poking around in the fountain across the street until he pulled the phone out of the pocket and dialed Lisa's number. It rang until he was about to switch off when the phone was picked up and a man's voice said, "Hello."

"I need to speak to Lisa."

"Well, uh," the man hesitated and Daniel thought that he heard a voice in the background. "Lisa's a little indisposed right now; she'll have to call you back."

"Just let me speak to my wife!"

"Later sport." Then whoever it was hung up. Daniel immediately dialed again, punching the buttons with such force that he almost put his finger through the phone. He was going to talk to his wife whether what's-his-face wanted him to or not. The man picked up the other line. "Look, Sport, I said that you would have to talk to Lisa later."

"No, you look, dammit! I want to talk to my wife!" There was silence on the other end and for a few seconds Daniel thought that the might be getting Lisa, but it became obvious that the man had hung up on him again. Daniel did just as he thought he would and slammed his phone down onto his desk with such force that a piece of it hit the ceiling and rolled off into a corner. The rest of the phone had hardly bounced off into the trash can before Daniel was out the door and stalking down the hall toward the exit. He told his secretary that he had the squirts, would be going home for the remainder of the day, and to tell the school provost and the basketball coach that he would talk to them in the morning.

As he tore out of the parking lot and left campus, he was going over what the man on Lisa's phone had said, as well as the things that he and Lisa had said and not said, done and not done in the previous year of their marriage. During that time he had not wanted to accept that what the man had meant by "indisposed" was happening. He hadn't wanted to accept the fact that Wade Burgess was right and that what the nagging voice that had been speaking to him on those long lonely nights where he lay in bed alone had been telling him was true: his wife, Lisa, was having an affair. As he left Welbourne County and headed into Davidson, then Randolph County, then south into Moore, he went over the facts in his mind, things that should have told him the truth that he was blind to. There was the fact that he never saw her anymore, and the fact that, when she was home, she was more concerned with work and talking about work and Mr. Collins and worried about their new bonus room rather than paying attention to him. She never let him even touch her anymore and she sure never dolled up for him like she did for Mr. Collins on these supposed "buying trips," which were nothing of the kind. How many would they have to go on in a year? One, two, three at the most. How many had there been just this year? He didn't know for sure, but it must have been half a dozen at least. As he hit the outskirts of Pinehurst, images were dancing in his mind of what Lisa and Mr. Collins had been doing when they were supposedly choosing merchandise with which Willow's Stores could overcharge their customers. "Indisposed" can mean a great many things.

Daniel knew the way to Pinehurst; he, the Mayor, Wade and Mitchell had driven down to see Tiger Woods play in the U.S. Open. Getting there was easy, but finding the Hampton Inn was a different thing. Lisa had given him the hotel address on the message that she left on the answering machine, but he still couldn't find it, and a good hour of driving around town lost gave him even more time to fume. He finally gave up, stopped at a Pantry to get directions, and found out that he was a scant mile away.

The front desk had no record of a Mr. Collins, so Daniel asked about a Lisa McDaniel; there was one room registered under her name. So they were sharing a room. So much for being discrete! The girl behind the desk said that the room was 427 and Daniel stomped off toward the elevator without saying anything further. He hit the button on the elevator and stood with his arms crossed, fingers drumming until the doors opened and he stepped inside. He was in the car with two women, one old, one young and a toddler who screamed the entire way to the fourth floor so, when Daniel got off, he had a headache to top off his foul mood. He almost ran to room 427 and pounded on it, wanting to get it all over with before he lost his nerve. The door was thrown open and a man stepped partially out into hall. He was Daniel's height and looked to be his weight as well. He had tan skin, blond hair and eyes as blue as his shirt, which looked expensive, complete with cuff links. His shirt was unbuttoned at the top. He reminded Daniel of an oversized Ken doll.

"You Collins?" Daniel snarled. "From the Willow stores?"

"Yeah, who wants to know?" Before either man could blink, Daniel's right hand shot out and punched Collins square in the nose. The entire scene seemed to freeze there for a moment with Collins sprawling out in front of Daniel, a large wash of scarlet pouring out of his nose, before the man hit the floor, his head bouncing hard off the carpet. Daniel stepped into the room and instinctively looked toward the bed. Lisa was there reclining decadently with her bare feet crossed in front of her. She was surrounded by papers, folders and three-ring binders. She was sucking on the rear end of a yellow highlighter and was staring into a laptop that was sat across her legs.

"Daniel, what in God's name are you doing!"

It was shame that grabbed Daniel by the scruff of the neck, hauled him back out into the hall and pushed him toward the elevator. The look on Lisa's face had been one of total shock, of disbelief at the awful thing that the loser she married had just perpetrated. The look on Collin's face wasn't anger or vengeance, like you would have thought, but shock, as if he were asking himself why this crazed person would want to hurt him.

Daniel tapped the call button for the elevator until it came. He was tapping the button for the ground floor and the doors had just began to shut when Lisa slipped in between them. She just stood there and stared up at him for a moment. Rather than look at her Daniel looked over her shoulder at his reflection in the doors. He looked like a puppy who had been kicked once too often. She reached up, put a hand tenderly on his cheek and pulled his face down toward her own.

"Was that really necessary?" Her voice was not scolding or mean like Daniel had expected it to be, but soft and tender and, when he looked at her, she was smiling like she could almost laugh at what he had done. "You know my boss is in his room bleeding into the sink?"

"Don't you mean your room?"

"No, his own."

"There aren't any rooms under his name."

"Well, if you want to be nosy, ask the clerk about a room registered under the name of Church that's Mr. Collins' secretary. She always makes his reservations and, for some reason, she always puts it under her own name. Why don't you tell me what you thought was going on in my room." Daniel couldn't answer; he could only look back at his reflection. Lisa put on hand on the side of his face and pulled it down again, this time kissing him tenderly on the lips. She took his other hand in hers and looked at his cut finger. It hadn't hurt; in fact, he had forgot the injury all together and hadn't dressed it that morning just absently leaving the bandages off after he took off the old ones. "How's your finger?"

"Fine," he said and she kissed his finger.

"You know, you should know me better than that." He couldn't answer her again, only nod. "I love you."

"I love you, too." His voice was quiet and she could barely hear it.

"Always will." He nodded again. "More than anything." He couldn't help smiling. That was something that she used to say when they had been dating and just after they had been married. He couldn't remember when he had heard it last. The door opened at the ground floor and Lisa hit the fourth floor button; then she pressed herself against him and he held her close.

"Just a little jealous, I guess," he said with his chin resting on her head. "It's just that I've missed you."

"Yeah, I know. I guess I have been losing myself in my work, but it's the first job that I've had with any responsibility. You know it's nice to be needed."

"You are needed. You always have been. I need you a lot more than Mr. Collins and Willows ever will."

"Like I said, it's good to know." The elevator stopped and the door slid open. She pushed away from him but kept her hands on his shoulders. "Mr. Collins told me that I could go on back home, but we do have a lot of work left to do and it is very important, but it'll be the last trip for awhile. I promise." Daniel forced a smile and nodded. The doors started to shut but Lisa stepped into the doorway and held them open. "I'll be home tomorrow and we'll have a little talk. Okay."

Daniel didn't verbally agree, but he stepped to her and kissed her. This kiss was long and satisfying and it healed what ailed Daniel inside and out. When he walked out of the Hampton, he had a spring in his step that had not been there when he came in and he was sure to stop at the front desk and thank the girl for helping him. The trip home seemed to take half the time that it took to drive down and he stopped for gas and went through the drive-through at Burger King, getting burgers and fries for himself and Jesus. He hoped that Jesus would be home, he had some good news for a change.

When Daniel got there he was surprised; in fact, he was somewhat shocked that Jesus wasn't there sitting on the couch with his glass of water, and Daniel's heart sank as if it were an old friend of many years or a wife that was absent. He went to the counter, pulled out his burger and took a bite before he looked at the answering machine. There were two messages: the first one was a hang up and the second one was silent for several seconds. He thought that it might be a hang up as well or some automated message, a telemarketer or politician, but then Jesus' happy upbeat voice came on and Daniel instinctively stepped toward the answering machine so he could make sure he heard it all.

"Yeah, Daniel, it's me. You know, last night we were talking about me having disciples? Well, if you want the job it's yours. Your first job, should you choose to accept it, is to come and pick me up. I'm at the police station and they're saying something about making bail.

XIV
Jailbirds

Marilyn Misenheimer had been in jail once before, and that was a misunderstanding, but the day that she was picked up for indecent exposure was a day that she would remember as the worst of her life. Against her better judgement she had met Mitchell at the park and let him lead her into the bushes and prove his love to her as, according to Mitchell and Dr. McCandless, men do physically as opposed to women who prove theirs emotionally. She wasn't comfortable with it. It was even more demeaning than the whole Cloud Nine stunt, and it made her feel like some little high school slut sneaking a quickie before she was due home for curfew. She went along with it, however, hoping that this would be it as far as Mitchell's fantasies went, or at least that the rest of them stayed within the confines of their own bedroom.

She had been lying there with her eyes closed. What was the advice that English mothers used to tell their daughters for their wedding night? "Close your eyes, grit your teeth, and think of England." Well, Marilyn had been thinking of the book she was reading. Then her mind had wandered to the supplement to Dr. Beck's *Architectural History of Welbourne County* that she was helping him write. Then on to countless ancestors, the Hessian, anything to pass the time quicker and try and drown out the sounds of the basketball game where some of Welbourne County's own citizens were happily playing a game with Muslim extremists. Those thoughts by themselves had been enough to occupy her mind for most of the time, until she had heard a noise like something landing on the ground nearby and, as she had opened her eyes, a basketball bumped into the side of her head. When she saw what it was, she practically begged Mitchell to stop, knowing that somebody would come looking for the ball and, thinking of all the individuals that she had seen playing basketball on her way in, she couldn't think of a one that she would want catching her in her present situation. Mitchell had not stopped, however, as much as his wife protested and only yelled, "Go away!" and "Don't come back here!" which Marilyn thought would only call attention to them rather than rectify the situation. She had begun pleading even more and even demanding; she had actually put her hands on his chest to push him off her when she had looked up to see one of the Muslims, the tall one, looking down at her with a look on his face like he was marching to war. All Marilyn could do was scream, then Mitchell screamed and the Muslim screamed, although Marilyn couldn't tell if it was a scream of terror or a war whoop. She rolled Mitchell off of her and took off running, blazing another way through the bushes rather than using the one that was already there. She hadn't known where she was going or what she would do when she got there, especially if the Muslim followed her, but she had to get away before both she and Mitchell got their throats cut, she hoped that Mitchell had followed her. She really didn't pay any attention as she passed the bleachers and the basketball court although she heard the shouts, the whistles and the catcalls. It was right about then that she started to feel the breeze on the front of her legs, her groin and her stomach and realized that Mitchell still had hold of her skirt and, by this time, he was just now leaving the bushes. By the time that she got to the parking lot behind the baseball field, she had calmed to a point. It was then that she saw the faces: the mothers who pulled their Little Leaguers out of her way and the men, the coaches and baseball dads who pointed, smiled and laughed like they had a dollar to slip into her garter. She had kept on running and, as luck would have it the lady's room was a bee line in front of her, and she had been able to make it in no time, run into a stall and lock the door.

It seemed like forever until she heard Mitchell's familiar gait on the damp concrete floor, but she opened the stall door and peeped out, just in case. They didn't say a word to each other. Neither one knew what to say. He only wrapped his shirt, which he had not had time to put on, around her waist, put a strong arm across her shoulders and led her out of the bathroom. She had expected the leering crowd, which had not dissipated by one child since she had been in there, and put a hand in front of her face like a shamed celebrity being hauled into court in front of the paparazzi. They had headed for Mitchell's truck and Mitchell had just started helping her in when the patrol car pulled up.

It was all a case of a bad situation getting worse, like a ball of yellow snow growing bigger as it barrels down a hill. Mitchell put her in the truck and then started talking to the sheriff's deputies.

Marilyn couldn't hear what they were saying, but she had a good view of Mitchell shouting and screaming and waving his arms and the deputies standing there, listening stone faced, their thumbs laced into their gun belts the way they do. A crowd, mostly jeering men, moved in close to listen and every once in awhile they would turn away and slap their knees or nudge each other. In what seemed like an hour, but in reality was a quarter that, the policemen, with Mitchell right behind them, his face crimson with anger, came around to the passenger side door. Marilyn thought that they were going to tell her that she was free to go, but instead she was hauled out like a common criminal, handcuffed under the pretense of it being procedure, and stuffed into the back seat of one of the patrol cars! Another eternity of waiting followed. This one was worse than the last because she was sitting in a police car, staring at the whole scene through a plexiglass shield covered with hand and fingerprints and flecks of a yellowish green substance that turned her stomach to even think of its origins. There was more shouting, more gestures, and more stone-faced listening, then Mitchell was cuffed and put into the car right beside his wife.

On the way to the police station one of the deputies, Marilyn thought that it was the one who was running for Sheriff, talked on a cell phone practically the whole trip and, when the officers were pulling the Misenheimers out of the cruiser, it was he who informed them that they were being charged with indecent exposure and public fornication. For Marilyn the trip was spent worrying first about their son, Martin, who would have been getting home from school right about then. It made Marilyn sick to think of Martin learning about this, which he surely would, seeing as how news traveled in Welbourne County even among the children. The first order of business was to make sure that he was taken care of while they got this matter all sorted out. The plan, if he was ever home alone and something came up, was to stay with Becky Lewallen next door and she guessed he could do that, but how long would he have to stay? Would Becky mind if he stayed late or spent the night? They had to get word to Martin or to Becky, but they only got one phone call. Was that between the two of them or each? Marilyn didn't know and Mitchell didn't either, grunting his answer to her as the car pulled up behind the Sheriff's department and the adjoining jail.

The deputies that brought them in were called right back out and a very nice young woman did their paperwork, fingerprinted them and took their mug shots. This was the cherry on the top of the proverbial sundae of Marilyn's degradation that day, but the deputy did let her call Becky and arrange for Martin to stay there. "For as long as it takes," Becky had said, and she hadn't known what had happened, or, at least, Marilyn hoped she didn't know.

The young woman let Mitchell use his phone call to arrange bail for them. He tried the Mayor at work and at home and didn't find him. He was about to call Wade Burgess but thought better of it. The thought of Wade stomping in, bellowing and throwing his weight around, either calling attention to the situation or getting himself thrown in the clink as well, didn't set with either Misenheimer, and they doubted that Daniel McDaniel would even agree to come down. So, instead, Mitchell tried the mayor's cell phone and then, when he didn't answer, Marilyn gave him Pheobe's number. The phone rang awhile, but Pheobe picked up eventually, sounding none too happy about it, and Mitchell had to practically beg and assure her that it was a desperate emergency before she would even put the mayor on. They learned later that, since Pheobe had learned of the mayor's plan for him and Mitchell to hook up with a couple of fun girls in Myrtle Beach, she had made him pay for it-physically, mentally and most of all financially. At the time of Mitchell's call, they had been at the same little lodge that they visited each autumn up near Lake Lure, which was, as Pheobe put it later, a preliminary trip. She was making plans for a rather costly jaunt to the Caribbean.

Pheobe softened a little when she heard of the Misenheimer's plight, allowed the Mayor to come bail them out and even came along herself. Whether she came out of the goodness of her heart or to gawk and watch the circus that was the wretched existence of Mitchell and Marilyn Misenheimer, Marilyn didn't know and she never asked.

XV
Favors All Around

When Daniel walked into the Sheriff's Department the word that would best describe the situation occurring there was bedlam. The front counter and office area was packed with people, shoulder to shoulder, and most appeared to be local reporters for the various media. The sheriff himself was standing in a rear corner talking to a circle of people with microphones, while a man held a large camera on him, the light of which was so powerful that it lit up the room like the noonday sun. There was a bevy of other people who were gathered farther back from the sheriff trying their dead-level best to either reach over those in front of them and get their microphones closer or to listen to what the sheriff was saying and paraphrase it into their notebooks. Farther back still were the sheriff's deputies and other staff and supposed experts, who were offering their two cents on the bust at the second meth-house to those reporters not important or not aggressive enough to get a word with the sheriff himself. On top of that, Daniel had to wade through an ocean of people at the counter who had legitimate business at the Sheriff's department and were being ignored by the departmental staff while the sheriff and his boys basked in the glory. Those people included Tony Dorsett, T.J., who was standing against the wall looking at the wanted posters, Rufus, Gene Pickard and Stanley Fisher as well the Mayor and his wife Pheobe, who were pressed up against the counter. The mayor was slapping the palm of one hand with his checkbook.

"Hey!" The mayor said like he was genuinely glad to see his old buddy and he took Daniel's hand and gave him that politician, ex-marine squeeze that popped all the joints in Daniel's fingers.

"Hey." said Daniel, trying to get his hand back from the mayor. "Who do you have to sleep with to get some service around here?"

"I don't know, but we've been here for a good half hour and I think that I'd show Rufus there a good time if it'd get us waited on. What brings you down here?"

"Oh, I'm trying to help out a friend."

"It wouldn't happen to be Mitchell, would it?"

"No," Daniel said, throwing the mayor a confused look. "Is he here, too?"

"Yeah, you haven't heard?"

"No I haven't." Before the mayor could tell Daniel the whole sordid tale a young woman in a sheriff's uniform went by the other side of the counter close enough for the mayor to reach over and tap her on the shoulder.

"Oh, hey, Mayor." The deputy, whom the mayor hadn't seen before, said with a surprised smile on her face. "You here for the Misenheimers?"

"Uh, yeah." Said the mayor. "Would you have 'em brought out and we'll settle this."

"Yes, just one moment."

"And say," the mayor added before she could get away, "Mr. McDaniel here needs some help, too."

"Yes sir, and how may I help you?"

"Yes, I have a friend that has been picked up and brought here. I want to make bail for him if I could.

"And his name?"

"Well, uh," Daniel glanced at the mayor and his wife, who looked to be a little too engrossed in his conversation. "He'll be going by the name of Jesus. He's a little guy with a beard, a little unkempt. He'll be wearing a Carolina Panther's raincoat, blue."

"Oh, yes, but for him you may have to talk to the sheriff." The deputy headed toward a back doorway, stopping to tap one of the deputies on the shoulder and whisper a few words to him, gesturing to Daniel. The deputy nodded and headed over toward the sheriff who was wrapping up his press conference.

"Say, that's the bum that Wade said he saw you hanging around with. What do you want to hang around with a thing like that for?" the Mayor asked.

"Like I said, he's a friend of mine."

"Oh, you're too good to bowl with us but you go hang around a piece of trash like that. What's been wrong with you lately?"

"There ain't nothing wrong with me. Like I said, he's a friend of mine. He's helped me out and now I'm returning the favor."

"Yeah, and what are getting yourself into?" asked Pheobe over her husband's shoulder.

"Well, I don't guess that would be any of your business now, would it?" Both the mayor and his wife got their mouths ready for a retort, but at the same time the deputy brought out Mitchell and Marilyn, along with their paperwork, to post bond and the sheriff bellied up to the counter to talk with Daniel.

"Mr. McDaniel, I'd like to have a word with you about this friend of yours." The Sheriff held open the swinging counter door to let the Misenheimers out and Daniel in. Daniel avoided the Misenheimer's gaze, as well as that of the mayor and his wife, and, as he passed them, he could hear them talking.

"He's not with us?" Mitchell was asking.

"No, he's picking up a friend."

"Who?"

"I'll tell you about it outside." Also, moving the length of the counter on their way to the sheriff's office Daniel could hear one of the other deputies talking to Rufus.

"Yeah," Rufus sounded unusually rattled for him, and Daniel had to look toward him as he followed the sheriff into a side hallway. "I'd like to report a missing person."

Daniel followed the Sheriff into his office, which was so cluttered with papers, folders and various other brick-a-brack that Dorsey had to remove a stack of leather-bound books from a chair and slide it toward the desk to give Daniel a place to sit down. The sheriff then weaved his way around his desk and dropped his considerable girth into an old-fashioned wooden desk chair that creaked and groaned under his weight.

"Let me get out the folder that I have on your friend here, Mr. McDaniel, if you'll give me just a minute." As the sheriff was leafing through a large stack of files on the desk in front of him, Daniel scanned the walls out of boredom. There was a very large trout and the head of a jack-o-lope on the left hand wall next to a window, and a picture of the sheriff with the President and another with Loretta Lynn on the wall behind the desk. In the picture with Bush the sheriff was in uniform; undoubtedly this was in his capacity as a law enforcement officer. In the Loretta Lynn picture he was wearing some sort of tacky beige suit and a Shriner's fez, obviously a convention of some sort. In between the pictures was a plaque with the Shiner's symbol on it commemorating Leo Dorsey's twenty years of service to the Shriners and to the Welbourne County community.

"Oh, here we are." The sheriff opened the folder and stared down at it for a moment. Then he pulled the head off of a red, white, and blue ceramic elephant that he had sitting on his desk, on the opposite corner from the infamous miniature electric chair, reached in and pulled out a cookie.

"Want one?" He held the jar toward Daniel who declined. "My granddaughter's selling cookies for the Girl Scouts and I just love these caramel clusters." The sheriff popped in another cookie and chewed while he put the elephant's head back on and brushed his hands together. "Okay, Mr. McDaniel." He glanced back down at the folder and then smoothed down his comb over with one hand. "What happened with your friend is that we approached a duplex at 712 S. Fitzgerald and took our position outside of each door. I had just started the count to bust the door down when it opened and two men, one Caucasian and one African-American, both in their late thirties, early forties shoved another man out the door. Then one threw what appeared to be a Bible at him and said something to the effect of; 'We don't need your preaching here. You need to get the Hell to church if you wanna give a sermon.' Something to that effect, and we took that moment to rush in. Now your friend could have run and, to tell you the truth, it wouldn't have hurt my feelings if he had, but he stuck around, kind of getting in the way and trying to talk to the suspects. We were hauling them out, cuffing them and laying them in the front yard, and he was hovering over them, trying to preach to them or talk to them or something so we finally cuffed him, too. We thought that it was kind of suspicious that he would want to stick around there, so we brought him in. We just haven't decided whether he should be charged or not and what with."

"He sort of fancies himself as a preacher."

"Yeah, I know. That was obvious and I've got no problem with preaching the word of the Lord, but the fact was that he was impeding a police operation so he could be looking at that at least. It's obvious, though, that he wasn't in cahoots with the fellas that we arrested and, talking to him, he doesn't really seem to belong there. I'm hesitant to charge him with anything drug related." He took this opportunity to pull out another cookie and pop it in his mouth.

"Well, I'll swear to the fact that he wasn't there making or buying or using drugs. I think that he saw that as a place where there are people who need to be reached, who need to hear the word, so to speak"

"Well, he's right there. I'm just wondering how he knew about it. How'd he know where to go?"

"He's just got a sense of these things."

"We got an anonymous tip that told us where to go. Do you think that he could have done it?"

"It's possible, I guess; his behavior is a little erratic at times."

"Uh huh. Uh huh." The sheriff was now leaning back in his chair with his hands laced over his belly. There was a trail of cookie crumbs running down his tie. The whole scene made him appear even fatter than he already was. "So how do you know this man and how long have you been associating with him?"

"Just a few weeks; he's been helping me at my house. I'm doing a little work, adding a bonus room, and he's been helping me out for room and board and something to eat, things like that."

"So he's been living with you?"

"Yeah, he just happened to come by when I had sort of an accident out where I was working."

"I see that you cut your finger. You know that looks a little nasty. You might want to keep a bandage on it."

"Oh, Oh well," Daniel had forgot about the cut and looked at his finger like a small baby first discovering its hand. "This was another accident. I stepped on a rake the other time. I'm a little danger prone."

"Umm hmmm. And he just happened to be coming along and helped you with that injury?"

"Yes, I took a hard whack on the nose."

"Yeah, it does look crooked." This was the first Daniel had heard of this and he started feeling his nose and looking around for a reflective surface to check this out when the sheriff leaned forward in his chair and got down to business. "Mr. McDaniel, the thing is that I'm very hesitant to just let him go scott free. So, if anything, I would have to release him into the custody of you or another person and, to tell you the truth, I am very hesitant to do that as well. Now he wasn't involved with the operation at the duplex, but I still want to know what he was doing there and, if he knew where it was, why he didn't inform the proper authorities, that is if it wasn't him who tipped us off. I also have half a mind to recommend him for a psychiatric evaluation. We both know that normal people just don't go 'round calling themselves Jesus and preaching in drug dens." The sheriff paused at this point to size up Daniel, lean back in his chair, and smooth down his comb-over, which had fallen into his eyes again. "And the thing is, I don't know you from Adam's house cat. Now I think that I remember your daddy, maybe I used to know him. Was he in the Shriners?"

"No, he was a mechanic at the county motor pool. He probably worked on your car at one time or another."

"There you go! I thought I knew him and I remember him to be a good enough fella, but, again, I don't know the first thing about you. Well, not enough to release a potential suspect into your custody. Now maybe, if there's somebody that I know who could vouch for you, we might be able to work something out." One name immediately came to mind, but Daniel rubbed the bridge of his nose between two fingers as he tried to think of somebody, anybody else; none came to mind that might carry the same amount of clout.

"I bowl with the mayor."

"Well now, Mayor Farley's word will definitely carry some weight. Do you want to come back tomorrow and have the mayor call me?"

"He just left I could probably get him on his cell phone. I don't want Jesus. I mean my friend to spend a night in jail."

"That's right nice. Don't get me wrong. I'm thinking of what's best for the community."

Yeah and it wouldn't hurt come election time either, Daniel thought as he reached into his pocket for his cell phone. Not finding it, he remembered his hissy of that afternoon.

"I don't have my cell phone."

"You can use my phone," the sheriff volunteered, pulling a sheriff's department Smoky Bear style hat off the phone and spinning it around. Daniel had to stop for a moment with the receiver pressed against his chest while he struggled to remember the Mayor's cell phone number. He always had it on speed dial or on his cell phone's memory, so he very rarely had to dial it, but this time, somehow, he was able to piece it together and dial the number. The phone rang several times before the mayor picked up.

"Mayor Farley speaking."

"Hey, Birddog, I need a favor." Daniel made the request, grit his teeth, and braced for the mayor's response. When it came, it was far from vicious but packed a punch all the same.

"So it's Birddog when you need a favor, is it? A little while ago it was mind your own business." Daniel could hear a woman speaking in the background, Pheobe, or maybe Marilyn Misenheimer. He was glad that he couldn't tell what she was saying.

"Look, Birddog, we've known each other a pretty good while," Daniel started. His dander was up and, against better judgment, he went on the offensive. "I have never asked you for diddly squat, unlike Mitchell or Wade or a lot of other people in this town. This is just a small favor; it isn't like you've got to come get me out of jail or anything." The fact of the matter was that Daniel had asked the mayor for such a favor, the time when Daniel had crashed his bronco through Old Lady Liddy Boumont's chicken coup and the mayor had produced, getting him out of a DWI charge. He expected the mayor to throw that back in his face, and he was desperately planning an answer for him but Birddog didn't even bring it up.

"Well, what is it?"

"The Sheriff needs somebody to vouch for me so they can release my friend into my custody."

"See, I don't understand why you care," The mayor responded. Daniel heard the woman's voice in the background again but, again, he couldn't make out what she was saying.

"I just can't explain it. I'm trying to help the guy out. He helped me with something and now I owe him a good turn and I'll owe you a big one, too. You name it and, if you want me to patch things up with Wade, I will. Whatever you want." There was silence on the other end for a good while and Daniel asked the silence if the mayor was still there.

"Now, after I hang up with you, I'm going to call Wade. We're going to get together at the lanes and work things out. You got me?"

"Yeah, I got you."

"Put the sheriff on." Daniel had to smile as he handed the phone to the sheriff who had just popped another cookie into his mouth and had to chew for a moment before he could say hello.

"Hello, Mayor. Sorry I missed you a little while ago." The sheriff twisted his chair around so that he faced the wall with the fish and the jack-o-lope. Daniel got up from his chair and began to pace the room or pace as much as the clutter allowed. "Yeah, boy, it was a circus. Well, thank you very much. I... Yeah, well, I like our chances. Okay." The sheriff listened for awhile, smiling broadly as if the mayor could actually see him. "Well, we all like to play the Good Samaritan sometimes. Yes. Well, he seems like a fine fellow. Okay. Yes. Thank you Mayor. Good bye." The sheriff hung up and he was a lot more cordial, almost happy. "The mayor says that you are a man of impeccable character, but that you have a little bit of a short fuse so you might want to work on that a bit, but I am going to release this friend of yours into your custody."

"Thank you"

"Now I want him to remain in Welbourne County. More than likely we'll want him for questioning, so he cannot leave the area and he's to stay with you. You are the responsible party. Got me?"

"Yes, sir thank you."

"You're welcome. Now let's go see if we can get your boy fixed up." The sheriff got up, popped another cookie into his mouth and made his way to the door. Daniel followed him back down the hall and into the office area. "Hey, Carrie!" The woman deputy who had been helping the mayor looked over from where she was talking to two young men with writing pads in their hands. "Get that little long-hair that we picked up in the bust this evening. We're releasing him into Mr. McDaniel's custody." The young woman nodded to the men and trotted off through a door in the other side of the room, the same one the Misenheimer's had been led through. The sheriff led Daniel to the counter and held the door open for him to step through while he stayed on the business side. "Now, Mr. McDaniel, I need you to sign this. There is no bail since he will not be formally charged, but I still need your signature saying that he is being released into your custody." Daniel signed and dated the form, glancing over the print but not really reading anything. When he looked up, the young woman was leading Jesus toward him. Jesus was smiling, as usual.

"Hey, Daniel, thanks for coming."

"Yeah you pop up in the strangest places." The young woman let Jesus out though the counter door.

"I'll see you boys later," the sheriff called after them. "And remember: don't leave the county."

"Okay," Jesus said.

"You're pretty lucky to have a friend like that you know?"

"Oh, yeah, everybody should have a friend like Daniel," Jesus said earnestly.

XVI
The Grocer

When Daniel and Jesus stepped out of the police station, it felt warm, almost hot, after having been in the air-conditioned Sheriff's department for so long. Daniel's day had already stretched years too long, and he made a bee-line for his truck, just wanting to get home, plop down on the couch and maybe watch a ball game. Just a few days previous, this ritual would have included a beer, unthinkable now. He turned around to tell Jesus that he had burgers at home, and maybe lay in a lecture about discretion being the better part of valor, but Jesus wasn't there. A slight surge of anger and then panic swept over Daniel at the thought of losing his charge, but he looked back toward the door and saw him across the parking lot talking to Tony Dorsett, Rufus and a couple of others. As Daniel looked their way, Jesus motioned him over.

"Purdie Mae's missing."

"Missing?" Daniel looked across the faces of the men Jesus was talking to and all looked worried. Rufus looked downright scared, and Daniel had never seen him flustered. He couldn't imagine anything rattling his cage after all those years dealing with Purdie Mae.

"Since about three, three-thirty this afternoon," Rufus said. His voice had a little quiver in it. This man was worried.

"Did you tell the police?"

"They said we'd have to wait twenty-four hours for an adult to be declared missing." Daniel thought for a second, looking across all the worried faces, back to Rufus' which, and Daniel didn't even know the man that well, was downright disturbing as to the amount of anxiety that further wrinkled an already wrinkled old face. He thought he had to say something, suggest something, anything, but Jesus beat him to the punch.

"Shouldn't we go look for her?"

"We already looked," Tony said from where he sat beside T.J. on his truck's tailgate.

"Well we could try again. Maybe she's back." Daniel could have headed this off and he probably should have. As he stood there listening to them talk, Sheriff Dorsey's voice came to his ears as the voice of reason. *Don't you do that boy. You keep an eye on him. He's your responsibility.*

"Maybe we could," said Rufus brightening a little at the thought of something that they could do.

"And we'll be one more car." Jesus patted Daniel on the back. "We can cover more ground." Daniel looked at everyone and they all looked at him, as if they were waiting for him to answer.

"Oh, what the Hell," Daniel said and winced at his choice of words. He looked at Jesus who seemed oblivious. "We don't have to be back anytime soon, but he can't leave the county." He stuck a thumb in Jesus' chest.

"That won't be no problem." Rufus managed a smile. "Purdie Mae hadn't been outta Welbourne County since she went down to Chesterfield to bail her Mama out of jail."

"Okay, where would she be?"

"The only place I can think of," Rufus began counting the choices off on his long pencil like fingers, "is the house and the restaurant and then we been checking the motel. That's where those terrorists been staying."

"Terrorists?" Tony gave Daniel the condensed version of the story which ended in the basketball game and Purdie Mae's mission to sneak into the back of the terrorists' van to try and find some evidence as to what they were doing in Welbourne County.

"Oh for the love of....." Daniel walked around in a circle in disbelief at hearing such an asinine story. He wasn't concerned about terrorists. Most likely the men were just passing through, basketball team or not, but you just couldn't be too careful these days. He was still worried that they might try to hurt Purdie Mae although the thought of anybody picking Purdie Mae Pearce as a potential victim was laughable even though she was in the back of their van and outnumbered. Daniel shook off his apprehensions. No matter how tough Purdie Mae Pearce was, she was still a human being and might need help. "Okay, like Jesus said, let's split up and cover the obvious first."

"I'll try at the house," Rufus volunteered and went toward his beat-up old Chevy parked on the other side of Tony's truck. Stanley went with him and as they got into the car the rest could hear him talking.

"You know, this smells an awful lot like some government plot to me. Did you hear...."

"I'm going to go back and check that motel again," Tony said as he slipped off of his tailgate and handed Daniel his business card. "Call me on my cell phone if you find her." He then put up the tailgate and T.J. slid up into the back of the truck in among hard drives, monitors and canisters of pesticide, another fantasy taking shape for him. He was Sonny Crockett behind the wheel of a high-powered speed boat, dressed in a white suit over a light blue t-shirt. Sitting beside him his father was a very light skinned Tubbs. Jan Hammer's synthetic theme song played in the background as they made their way down a long canal in Miami, scanning the banks for the governor's missing daughter.

"I guess that leaves us to check the restaurant." Daniel scanned the lot to see who was left as he put Tony's card into his breast pocket. Only Jesus, Gene and himself remained. Daniel motioned for the other two to follow and hurried toward the truck.

"You know, Daniel," Jesus beamed as he walked just behind him. "You sure are a good person."

"Yeah, I'm a regular Billy Graham."

"Mama met him once," said Gene as Daniel unlocked one of the backseat doors and opened it for him.

Jesus and Gene talked about Mama's trip to Charlotte where she got to shake Billy Graham's hand and chattered on about this and that until Daniel turned onto Patton Ave. They both kept silent as Daniel crept down the street toward the Poultry Palace and Gene let out a loud gasp as they crested a slight rise and the orange van could be seen parked in front of the restaurant.

"That's their van," Gene whispered as they pulled to a stop several feet behind it. "What are we going to do?"

"I'm going in," Daniel said immediately, almost comically like the hero in a bad action movie.

"What if they're in there?" Gene whined as they stood on the sidewalk and gazed pensively at the light coming through the restaurant's front window. "They might be armed and there's no telling what they'll do to us." Daniel thought for a minute and then went to the toolbox that sat across the truck's bed. He searched for several minutes and finally produced a ball peen hammer for himself and handed Gene a roofer's knife which had a sharp curved blade every bit of three inches long. Gene held it out in front of himself like someone would weld a toothbrush or maybe a candle on a dark night. Daniel turned to Jesus and tried to think of something to give him as a weapon, but Jesus was already making his way up the sidewalk to the door. Daniel and Gene caught him just as he was about to walk past the big picture window adorned with the name of the restaurant and a chicken wearing an apron and pulled him back, plastering themselves against the wall. Daniel told them to stay where they were, got down on his hands and knees, crawled to the window and peered inside. He could see a small man, dark skinned, obviously Middle-Eastern, wearing a green warm-up suit, sitting at the counter, holding something against his head. Purdie Mae was standing nearby mopping the floor, dancing around like all was normal. Daniel stared at them for awhile, closing his eyes for several seconds and then opening them. The scene stayed the same and, standing up, he grabbed Gene and Jesus by the front of their shirts and dragged them to the window.

"This doesn't look like a hostage situation to me." By then Purdie Mae had already seen them and had made her way to the door.

"Hey, what are ya'll doing messing around out there?" she said, leaning out the doorway.

"Looking for you," Gene said walking toward her. "We thought the terrorists got you."

"Terrorists! You know ya'll are about stupid. Come on in here." She held the door open for them and, as Daniel passed by her, she looked at him and grinned. "Caught you up in all this too, huh?" Daniel could only nod his head and blush. After she had closed and locked the door, Purdie Mae walked by him and pointed at the hammer. "What you gonna do with that? You gonna knock 'em in the head, are you?" Daniel threw the hammer down on the table and stood in front of it as if trying to hide it. Purdie Mae cackled as she walked to the little man at the counter. He still had his bead bowed although he looked around at all of them. His lip was badly swollen, a trickle of blood was running down his chin and, when he raised his head and looked around, he had scratch marks down each cheek; a chunk of his hair had been yanked out at one temple.

"So they ain't terrorists?" Gene asked blankly, looking at the man as if he were a hamster in a cage. The man rolled his eyes and pushed his face down into the ice wrapped in a damp cloth that he cradled in one hand. "If they ain't, what're they doing here?"

"They're a basketball team, just like they told you they were."

"You're kidding."

"No, said Tater, tossing the rag onto the counter beside a basket bearing a half-eaten hamburger, "It is just as we said. We are a basketball team. We are not terrorists. Your country is supposed to be so enlightened, but no one can be a Middle Eastern man without being suspected as a terrorist."

"I need to find the phone and let them know where you are," Daniel stated as he walked to the counter to join them.

"On the wall." Purdie Mae pointed with her head. Daniel called Tony and told him that they had found Purdie Mae at the restaurant. Tony said that he would find Rufus and they would be there shortly. As Daniel got back to the group, Gene was asking Purdie Mae what happened.

"Well, I got into the back of their van easy enough and started fishing around in there. Didn't find anything, some clothes, basketballs, bunch of other stuff but nothing like bombs or poison or anything like that. There was a gun in there, but, shoot, tell me who in Welbourne County doesn't have a gun in their car." *Me* thought Daniel as he had been wishing he had one outside the restaurant.

"I had gone over the whole van and was going over it again when they got back and I couldn't get out without them seeing me, so I hid behind the box for that basketball goal that they bought at Brown's the other day. I figured they would go to the motel, or somewhere else, and leave the van. Then I could slip out and call ya'll to come get me, but they didn't get out; they just rode around arguing and jabbering at each other, yelling and screaming. They finally got back to the Cloud Nine and got out of the van, but they stood outside yelling some more. When they finally got through, I waited, must have been thirty minutes, and stood up to get out when the back door opened and the squirt here climbed in. I tried to make up some excuse, but he started screaming at me, babbling and jabbering, pushed me down, slapped my face so I had to whip his ass for him." She gestured to Tater, who presented his face as evidence. "And I made him bring me back here and we've been having a long talk. What do ya'll want to eat?" Before anyone had a chance to answer, Rufus and Stanley showed up outside the door, unlocked it and burst in.

"Where in the hell have you been?" Rufus yelled in a tone that was more accusatory than worried.

"I been battling terrorists," Purdie Mae said sarcastically, gesturing to Tater who went back to eating his hamburger. She told her story again for them and then again when Tony and T.J. got there, all the time cooking everyone supper and Tater dessert. They had eaten in silence for a good while before Tony wiped his mouth and began trying to strike up a conversation with Tater, more for an apology than anything else.

"So what happens now?"

"What do you mean?"

"Well, are ya'll still playing Wake Forest?"

"We cannot. There is no we. My men have left. When the woman heard us arguing, I was berating them for playing so poorly and they began arguing with me. The disobedient fools, they began yelling back at me, blaming me, saying that my performance was worse than their own, especially Bubba, which was such a shock. He was always my best, the most obedient. Anyway they have all left; there is no more team. No more game with Wake Forest, no more glory for Yeman, no more glory for Tater."

"So where are you going to go now?"

"Back to Yeman. I will go back in disgrace, but I will beg Allah for forgiveness. My uncle is a grocer in our capital city of Sana. Perhaps I can work for him."

"Well, I guess God needs grocers and cooks as much as he needs warriors and basketball players," Rufus stated. Tater grunted, wiped his mouth and slid off his stool. "I am leaving your city now."

"I guess we all owe you an apology." Tony started to put out his hand but Tater passed by him and left the restaurant without saying anything further.

He got in his van and started the engine. As he pulled away everyone in the restaurant heard him scream. "INFIDELS!"

As Jesus and Daniel pulled into the McDaniel's driveway, Jesus pulled his pack onto his lap. Daniel hadn't even noticed that he had it with him.

"Going somewhere?"

"I'm moving on. I think I'm needed somewhere else."

"No, you remember what the sheriff said; you need to stay in the area."

"Nothing's going to come of that Daniel. I'll guarantee you won't hear another word about it." Daniel thought that he ought to argue, that he ought to put his foot down and he probably should've, but he didn't. He knew that there wouldn't have been any use and he didn't want to argue.

"Won't you stay tonight and leave in the morning? It's kind of late."

"No, I better head on. You have company tonight." He pointed toward the house and, for the first time, Daniel noticed that Lisa's car was in the driveway. When he looked back toward him, Jesus was already several steps toward the road.

"Thank you," Daniel called after him.

"Thank you, Daniel," Jesus called back to him. "Thank you."

When Daniel got to the door Lisa was standing in the doorway. She was dressed a lot like she had been when she had last left. Daniel had never seen her look more beautiful.

"How's your boss?"

"He'll live, but I think you broke his nose."

"Uh-oh."

"Yeah, but he's not pressing charges."

"That's good."

"Do you know how stupid that was?"

"Yeah, I know. Still love me?"

"More than anything." Lisa put her arm around her husband's waist as they walked into the kitchen. "I picked up a six-pack on the way. You want a beer?"

"No, thanks."

XVII
J

The next day Bubba and Skeeter went back to the Cloud Nine Motel and checked in, requesting the same room that they had shared with the rest of the team. They retrieved the materials that they had hidden above a panel in the ceiling, unbeknownst to Tater and the rest. They used those materials to make a bomb which they mailed to the Raleigh office of Senator T. Don McFarland. The plan had been well thought out by Bubba and those men who had trained him, concocted the plan, and arranged for him and the rest to make their way into the U.S.A. to strike at its formerly thought safe southern states. The plan was well thought out except for the fact that Skeeter had not included enough postage and the package was returned. Upon receiving the package and not being able to read his own illegible handwriting, Skeeter opened it and obliterated half of the motel, killing himself and Bubba, but, fortunately, no one else. The explosion was investigated by the Welbourne County Sheriff's department until it was taken over by the F.B.I.. After a year-long investigation, it was concluded that the explosion was retaliation by a jealous husband who learned that his wife had been meeting a lover at the Cloud Nine. Sheriff Leo Dorsey and the investigating deputies signed a confidentiality agreement to never tell what they really found at the Cloud Nine and to swear from that point on that the explosion was not terror related.

Tater drove to New York where he planned on catching a plane to Frankfurt and then flying on to Yeman from there. In Germany his plane was hijacked, destination: Washington, D.C. but it was forced down in London. His current whereabouts are unknown.

June Bug and Skillet made their way to San Franciso where they became life partners, opened a woman's clothing store and joined the Republican Party of California. In April of 2003 they were beaten to death at a peace rally when, noting the elation of the Iraqi people at the fall of Saddam Hussein's regime, made the assumption that the invasion of Iraq may have been a good idea.

Mitchell and Marilyn Misenheimer pleaded guilty to a lesser charge and were let off with a stiff fine. They fired Dr. McCandless, bought 1957 Chevrolet and restored it together. They take the Chevy to car shows throughout the state and, if you're ever through Welbourne County and see a Cherry Red '57 Chevy polished until it sparkles and sporting a license plate that reads THE HESSIAN, that's them.

Sheriff Leo Dorsey was re-elected to the post of sheriff. His opponent, Kevin Miller, withdrew his bid for the office when he was arrested in a raid on a whorehouse out on Commanche Road.

The attempt at reuniting the Birddog Realty bowling team did not go well. Wade did not accept Daniel's apology and made it known that it was either Daniel on the team, or himself. Not both. It was Daniel who chose to walk away. Birddog Realty came one pin short of winning their seventh straight league championship. The team who beat them, The Four Horsemen, won the final game

largely due to their newest member, Daniel McDaniel, who picked up five straight 6-10 splits.

Daniel and Lisa spent the next weekend in Wilmington courtesy of Mr. Bernard Collins. When they returned home, Daniel found his Carolina Panthers raincoat hanging on the backdoor doorknob. There was a piece of notebook paper rolled up in one pocket with a note scrawled across one side:

Dear Daniel,

I just wanted to let you know that you're a good disciple. I've had better, but I've had worse and I am proud to know you. You're a good man, Daniel McDaniel, and we'll see each other again one day. You can be sure of that.

J.